The Golden Bird

The
Golden
Bird

SHANNON GARST

Illustrated by PANOS GHIKAS

1 9 5 6

HOUGHTON MIFFLIN COMPANY   BOSTON

The Riverside Press Cambridge

The Riverside Press

CAMBRIDGE • MASSACHUSETTS

PRINTED IN U.S.A.

wyo

contents

1   The Big Wish   1

2   Forbidden Adventure   16

3   Off to Earn a Burro   25

4   Diablo   33

5   A Wish Gone Wrong   41

6   A Useful Friend   50

7   Lucio Steals a Bride   56

8   Time of the Evil Eye   68

9   The Great Adventure   79

10   Lost!   88

11   Where Am I?   99

12   Strange New World   111

13   A Fork in the Trail   123

14   A Dream Come True   131

To KENT and JANIS SPURLOCK

In memory of our happy visits to Mexico

The Big Wish

Tara stopped beside the narrow trail and stood to one side when he heard the familiar *click, click* of sharp hoofs on the hard ground. Tlaka, Tara's spotted dog, squatted against his leg and growled.

"Quiet, Tlaka." The boy put a hand on the dog's head. "It is only a burro train."

Around the bend came four burros with flat pieces of leather and dangling ropes across their backs. A man rode the largest burro. His eyes were closed and his head bobbed on his chest. Tara smiled to see him taking his siesta while riding. A boy about Tara's own age rode the rear burro, sitting so far back that it was a wonder he did not slide off. He gave Tara a flashing grin and shouted, *"Hola!"*

"Hola." Tara grinned too and stood watching until the little train was out of sight past another bend of the winding trail. No doubt the boy and his father were from one of the tiny Mexican fishing villages beside the big lake and they were on their way into the mountains to gather fuel. Tara had seen this sight

many times and could picture the burros on their return carrying such loads of wood that the piles looked as though they were trotting along by themselves.

The sight of the boy sitting so happily astride the burro brought back the big wish to Tara's heart. And as he stood there in the shade of the jungle-like trail the wish grew and grew until it became a huge ache. Finally Tara sighed and continued his journey, but more slowly now, for his feet had become so heavy that his bare toes scuffed up little puffs of dust.

Where the thick trees and undergrowth ended he stepped into the bright glare of the hot sun. There before him lay the big lake like a jewel circled by mountains. Its waters flashed and sparkled in rich shades of blue and turquoise. He drew in his breath at the beauty of the sight as he always did. Although he saw it nearly every day, it never appeared twice the same.

Anxiously his eyes searched the shoreline, then he gave a small cry of happiness. Lucio was there, bent over the dugout canoe he was making from a log. Lucio was Tara's uncle — a young man grown, who had seen much of the world and was handsome and wise beyond belief, yet who was kind and friendly to his young nephew.

Tara broke into a run. "I was afraid you would be out on the lake," he panted as he came up beside Lucio.

Lucio straightened up, rested a sturdy leg on the prow of the canoe, and stretched his strong arms. He wore nothing but a pair of short white pants rolled up as high as they would go. Sweat glistened on his brown skin as he stood there outlined against the blue sky. Tara was reminded of the stories he had heard of his own Tarascan ancestors, who were tall and handsome as gods and had long ago run the many miles from this very lake to place on Montezuma's breakfast table whitefish still steaming hot.

Lucio wiped the sweat from his forehead with the back of his hand and returned to work. Tara picked up a sharp rock and also began scraping the charred wood to hollow the inside of the dugout.

"When this boat is finished," Lucio said, "I will take you with me to shoot the ducks. Someday, when you get bigger, I will make you a butterfly net of your own so you can catch the delicious whitefish."

Tara grinned up at his uncle and scraped harder and faster for a while, then his motions became slower and slower. His thoughts drifted far away. Today his heart was not in this work, in spite of Lucio's promise of exciting adventures on the lake.

"What is it, young nephew?" Lucio's voice broke into Tara's dreams. "I noticed when I first looked at you this morning that your black eyes looked like pools in the mountains — deep with longing — or trouble. And when you smiled your lips closed too quickly over your teeth. Tell me about it."

Tara straightened up and a giant sigh came from him. "Did you ever want something so much it hurt in here?" He put both hands over his stomach.

Lucio nodded. He always understood. "Tell me what this big want is that makes you hurt inside." In his voice there was not that laughter or teasing note which grownups often use when speaking to children.

"I want a burro. A burro of my own. I want a burro so much that I feel sick with wanting." The words spilled fast from Tara's lips.

"That is a big wish for a boy." Lucio stopped working to talk about this great problem. "Your good father owns a burro. He lets you ride sometimes."

"But Toto is not mine. He is the family's. The burro I want must belong to me. Be my very own."

Lucio nodded. "I know how you feel. But why must you have a burro of your own?"

"I want to go to faraway places. I want to ride over the whole world. I want to see everything there is. I even want to go to Mexico City."

Now Lucio threw back his head and laughed. But it was kind, not hurting laughter.

"Well I understand how you feel, Restless One," he said. "When I was a boy I, too, wanted to see the whole world — even Mexico City." His face sobered. "But I longed for something that would carry me even faster than a burro. I felt that I could not live until I owned a bicycle."

Tara's eyes widened. "Only the rich young men in Mexico own bicycles!" he cried.

He went back to scraping the charred wood, but his movements were slow. A bicycle! Such a fine means of getting about the world was far beyond his wildest dreams. A burro was the most he could ever hope for.

"I am not rich, yet I once owned a bicycle." Lucio's tone was proud. "I was much older though than you are now."

"How did you get it?"

Lucio looked at his young nephew as though surprised at the question. "Worked for it, of course. How else does a Tarascan Indian get what he wants? We do not beg or steal as so many of our shameless neighbors do."

Tara nodded. "But how did you earn so many pesos? It could take a lifetime to earn enough to buy a bicycle — even a burro."

Lucio chuckled and flexed the muscles of his brown arms. "I am strong," he said. "I worked hard for many, many turns of the sun. On the coffee and banana plantations. Following the wooden plow after the oxen in the dusty fields. Stooping over to plant the corn. Tramping the wheat. Anything I could do to earn a few pesos. And finally I had enough to buy a bicycle from a friend who was tired of seeing the world. Then I set out to see everything. Even the City of Mexico. And there, my Restless One, is the world itself. You need go no farther. Everything is there."

Tara thought with longing of the wonders ahead that he must see someday.

Both of them bent to work on the dugout once more

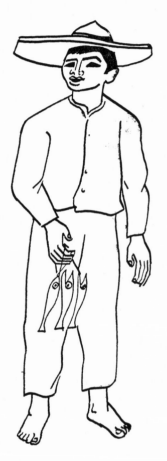

and as they scraped Lucio told him of the strange and marvelous things he had seen — the adventures he had had when he owned a bicycle.

At last Lucio straightened up and slapped Tara on the shoulder. "My stomach tells me it is time for eating *tortillas,*" he said heartily. Then he stood off to view their work. "I think it will do. Tomorrow, if you are in a reckless mood we will go on the lake and see how she rides. And maybe shoot some ducks for a fine feast."

"I will be here when the sun comes up," Tara cried.

"Later will do as well." Lucio smiled down at him. "Run home now. Take these whitefish to your good mother to cook for your supper." He lifted a string of fish from the water's edge, where he had put them to keep cool.

"You are kind." Tara took the string and smiled his thanks to this big uncle who was his hero.

On the way home Tara met Pepe, his best friend. Pepe's dark brown eyes were dancing with excitement as the boys faced each other on a corner of the small village square.

He thrust a hand into his pocket and drew out five coins which he jingled gleefully. Then with a big grin he drew out a crumpled bill which he waved beneath Tara's nose.

"*Touristas* came to the village today," he said. "They were big of heart. Much cincos. And even a peso for carrying a *tourista's* purchases to the boat. Why do you never come to the square with me, Tara, when the *touristas* come? If you would look at the *americano* women with those big soft eyes of yours they would toss handfuls of cincos to you."

At Pepe's remarks something within Tara cringed. He did not blame Pepe for begging from the Americans. It was a practice of most boys, both Indian and Mexican, these days. But Tara did not beg from anyone. He was descended from Tarascan kings, and the thought of having money thrown at him was revolting. These feelings, however, were things he could not explain to Pepe.

"But," Pepe went on in a condescending manner, "you must learn to speak Spanish and English. I learn

Spanish in school and English I pick up from the *americanos.*"

Tara nodded. Pepe was forever jabbering away in Spanish and using a few English words in his show-off manner.

"I'd like to speak Spanish," Tara said. "I can understand much of what is said, but I can't speak it very well. My parents talk only the Tarascan."

Pepe said, "You do not go often enough to the market place of the big village. Many people speak Spanish there."

Begging was a characteristic Tara did not like in his friend. Otherwise, though, they had fun together, roaming the hills, tending their goats, playing marbles, having pretend bullfights, or tossing stones into a small hole.

Pepe, like many of the village boys, went to the *escuela* — the school where he learned to speak Spanish and to make black marks on paper and to read from books. Tara, like most Indian boys of the mountains, did not go to school. For one thing, his grandfather, the Wise One, held out against the new ways. Nor did Tara have any wish to be cooped up inside a building for long hours, although he did envy Pepe's ability to read the black marks in books. Those marks, Pepe said, told of many wonderful things and Tara had a great curiosity about the strange world outside the little village.

In other ways, though, Tara felt sorry for Pepe, because he did not enjoy the freedom of being a mountain boy.

"I must hurry home with the whitefish Lucio gave me," Tara said, "so that my mother can cook them for supper."

Tara ran through the little village where pigs, dogs, and chickens scurried before him. Tlaka barked at every animal, making a great noise. They entered the narrow trail that led steeply uphill to the huddle of straw-roofed adobes where Tara's family lived.

He went into the shadowy room in which the cooking was done. There was no glass over the one window, and thick vines shut out most of the light. No one was there, but a tiny fire of corncobs smoldered under the stone on which the *tortillas* were cooked — a stone standing on three rocks, the same rude stone upon which *tortillas* had been roasted by Tara's ancestors for hundreds of years.

He put the fish beside the little stove and looked around the familiar room with its bright pottery on two rude shelves — at the large *ollas,* or water jugs, so beautifully decorated, at the reed sleeping mats rolled and standing in the corner. As always, the familiar things gave him a feeling of warmth and comfort.

He went outside to get some leaves to cover the fish so that the flies would not get on them. Cheran, his mother, was coming up the trail with a large water jug on one shoulder. Marina, his sister followed, with the new baby, Chiqua, cradled in her dark *rebozo*.

"I brought a string of whitefish Lucio gave me," Tara called out.

"That is good," his mother said, smiling. "Go to the adobe of the Wise One and tell him and the Good One to eat with us."

Marina ran to join him, Chiqua bouncing on her back as she ran. Tara chuckled at the sight. Marina was younger than he was, yet he could scarcely remember seeing her without a baby wrapped in her *rebozo,* either on her back, or cradled in her arms. Mexican or Indian girls were baby tenders from the time they were old enough to carry an infant. Yet, most of the native babies died before they were a year old and Tara, Marina, and the little doll-like Chiqua were the only living children of the eight born to the Olina family.

Tara peered into the shadowy room where his grandfather and grandmother worked. Zolic the Wise One was busy, as usual, with his paints and lacquers. His work was famous in the markets of the nearby city

— in fact over the whole state of Michoacán. The secret of his workmanship had been handed down from father to son through every generation since long before the hated Spanish conquest of Mexico.

The Good One, Tara's grandmother, had come from a famous family of weavers. Her beautiful serapes and *rebozos* were nearly as famous as the Wise One's lacquer ware, although it seemed that the skill of weaving was more common than the special ability it took to paint beautiful figures on gourds and wooden plates and bowls.

"I give you good evening," Tara said. "You are to eat fish with us."

Both withered old faces turned toward him and smiled. Tara felt enveloped in the warmth of their love.

"It is good!" the Wise One said. "First I must finish putting the lacquer on this gourd — then we will be along."

When Tara turned away from their door he saw Chalma, his father, come down the path from the mountain driving Toto, the gray burro, so loaded with firewood that only his nose and hoofs showed.

Tara sighed at the sight, remembering his great wish. If he had a burro of his own he could help get the wood and carry things to and from the market. Then betweentimes he would ride out to see the world.

He stepped up to assist his father in loosening the ropes that held the wood. It fell with a loud clatter.

Tara reached up to the limb of a nearby tree and got
the hobble, which he put around Toto's front legs to
keep him from wandering too far away.

The good smell of cooking fish and *tortillas* came
from the little adobe with the giant wisteria draping
its graceful blooms over the front door. Cheran and
Marina knelt beside the stone stove picking up little
balls of ground corn meal and slapping them from
hand to hand until they were flat cakes ready to be
roasted on the hot stove. These were the *tortillas*
which formed the main part of every meal.

The grandparents came hobbling over, arm in arm.
Each one used a knobbed stick as a cane.

Zolic the Wise One had a strong, rugged face and
his eyes reminded Tara of a hawk's, although they
could turn soft and gentle when the mood was on the

ancient man. He was the leader of the village near which the Olina family lived. Whenever anyone was in trouble, or needed advice they always came to Zolic, who had the wisdom of many years. In his veins flowed the proud blood of the Tarascans — the only Indian race in Mexico that had fled to the mountains rather than submit to slavery or the will of the conquering Spanish so many years before.

The tiny village on the shore of the lake had once been the capital of the Tarascan kingdom. Now times were changed. There were no longer any Tarascan kings, and "the Place of the Humming Birds," which had once been the capital, was now but a simple, serene fishing village on the lakeshore. Since no roads led to it, it was cut off from the rest of the world except by boat.

Zolic liked it this way. He held out for the old ways and hated to see the changes that were coming to his world.

Tara picked up a fish by the tail and, putting back his head, let it slide into his mouth. Then he used a *tortilla* to scoop up brown beans cooked for a long time in a sauce made of tomatoes and chile. His hunger slightly satisfied, he told about the new kind of boat Pedro, one of Lucio's friends, had on the big lake. It was larger than a dugout canoe and had some kind of machinery in it which made it skim over the water without any oars. It had already taken tourists to the fishing island where loomed the giant white statue of

José Morelos, one of the heroes of Mexico's fight for
independence.

Zolic frowned and shook his head over this bit of
news. "The old ways are best. The new ways — the
money of the *americanos* are corrupting our people."

There was scarcely a day that Tara did not hear
this remark from the Wise One.

Cheran would have liked to allow Tara to go to
school, but Zolic had raged against this idea. "The
new ways are making our people lazy," he cried. "Making beggars of them. Soon they will turn to thievery,
as many of our neighbors have done."

"Pepe knows boys who are learning to pick the
pockets of the rich *americanos*," Tara said between
bites. "The boys crowd around the tourists when they
are in the market. They say it is easy. Some even
snatch the handbags of the ladies."

"I will listen to no more such talk!" Zolic shouted.

"You will do well to stay far away from these boys,"
Chalma said. Tara's father was a silent, grave man
who seldom spoke, but when he did his words bore
weight. "Such things as you just said, make my heart
sick."

"We are Tarascans," the booming voice of the Wise
One went on. "Tarascans do not steal, or cheat, or
beg. We work hard to hold to the old ways, which are
best. We make the things which we and our neighbors
use in our daily living. And into our handiwork we
create beauty so that our hearts may be glad while we

use the things our hands have shaped. It is better to barter what we have made for something we need that is made by our neighbors. This thing called money only causes unhappiness — breeds envy and greed, which bring evil into men's lives."

"But father sometimes goes to the banana and coffee plantations to work for pesos — money — " Tara said.

Chalma's mild voice broke in. "Just when I need to buy a young burro — or some other thing for which we cannot barter our lacquer ware or the weaving our women do. I agree with the Wise One. The old ways are best."

Tara reached over to lift a hot whitefish from the stone. He wrapped it in a *tortilla* and bit off a piece. His father's words had put a new thought into his mind. According to Chalma's reasoning, it was all right to go onto the plantations to work for money to buy a young burro. Perhaps this was the way to get his wish. Perhaps he was strong enough to work on a plantation. Perhaps he could earn enough to buy a brown burro.

Forbidden Adventure

Tara was beside the turquoise lake early the morning after the dugout canoe was finished. But Lucio did not come and did not come. Other men appeared with their darts for shooting ducks or their butterfly fishing nets rolled on long sticks. They climbed into their dugouts one by one and used their spoon-shaped paddles to shove off from shore.

At last all of the fishermen and duck hunters were on the lake in their canoes and Tara was left alone.

He scowled as he looked first toward the village to see if Lucio was on the way, then out on the water where the boatmen were becoming small and shadowy figures.

Lucio liked to meet the day at an easy gait — he did not rush to greet it headlong as Tara did. The boy knew this, but he was growing impatient. If Lucio did not come soon, all the ducks would be shot — or frightened away.

The dugout he and Lucio had finished yesterday lay at the edge of the lake, the water slapping its end. Tara put his hands against the boat and shoved with all his might. He puffed and grunted. After a time the dugout moved slightly. Tara sat down panting until he could get his breath. Then he started to move again.

Now the dugout was farther into the water, its bottom against the mud, where it slid easily. Finally it was out far enough. Tara jumped into it and picked up the spoon-shaped paddle. With it he pushed the clumsy little canoe free of the shore, onto the smooth water. He continued to shove the paddle spoon against the bottom of the shoreline until he was past the reeds. Now he could look down into the murky water and see hundreds of water snakes.

He tried to use the paddle the way he had seen Lucio do many times, but it was difficult for him to handle it. The paddle was too large and he was awkward. After struggling for some time he began to get the knack of it. At first he was inclined to travel in a circle, but by using the paddle now on one side and then on the other he made a little headway.

A thrill of triumph rushed through him when he realized that he could manage the canoe and make it go wherever he wanted.

This was fun! He wished that Chalma were a fisherman. It would be pleasant to set out in a boat each day with one of the butterfly fishing nets. It would be sport to scud back in a race with the other fishing boats when the day's work was done. Although Tara knew that his grandfather and parents planned to hand on to him the secrets for their beautiful lacquer ware, at the moment fishing seemed to him a far more exciting way of making a living. He sighed as he thought of the hours he would have to sit cross-legged wielding a little brush made from dog hair, or rubbing the colors in with his fingers and the palm of his hand. Tara, in his mind, made a bargain. He would be both lacquer-maker and fisherman and thus satisfy his parents and himself.

He could see the yellowish butterfly nets now, flashing like transparent wings in the sunlight. The great nets were double and fastened to long poles. When held upright they looked like giant, filmy butterflies. Now there were six canoes in a circle and the nets were being lowered without making a ripple in the water. Tara knew that the nets would be let down in such a way that a great circle of them was formed beneath the water where a school of fish had been sighted. When the fish "stampeded," they would find themselves neatly caught in the nets, lifted to the surface, and dumped into the dugouts.

Tara wanted to get closer to see better, so he changed from a sitting to a kneeling position. In his hurry he tipped the canoe dangerously. Tara grabbed the sides with both hands and shifted his weight to right the clumsy boat. He dropped the paddle in his fright. He was well out on the lake with no way to propel the dugout!

He tried paddling with his hands, but could make no progress. When the canoe tipped, several inches of water flowed in. But it was a warm day and sitting in water was not too uncomfortable. Yet in a very short time merely sitting there in the hot sun waiting for help became very monotonous.

He rose to his knees — very cautiously now — and shouted, waving his hands; but the butterfly fishermen were rolling their nets and moving on to another spot.

Tara yelled with all his might. One of the men turned, evidently saw him, and waved. He must have thought Tara was sending him a friendly greeting. The group scudded farther away and were finally out of sight. Tara sat there feeling himself the loneliest, unhappiest boy in the world. Why hadn't he had sense enough to wait for Lucio? What would his uncle think of him for going out in the dugout alone?

How would he ever get to shore? If he were missed, no one would think to look for him on the lake. He might sit here and starve to death. Or a terrible storm might come and capsize the canoe and drown him. Or at night monsters of the deep water might reach out and devour him. There was no limit to the wild and terrible ends he was able to imagine for himself.

The sky darkened and the sun hid its face. A chilly wind came up and cold rain began to pelt him. Afternoon squalls often rose suddenly on the lake and fish-

ermen hurried for shore before they hit. Tara hugged
himself with his arms and huddled in deepest misery.
Now that the sun was hidden, the water looked cold
and dirty and the thought of snakes made him shudder.
The depths of the water might hold giant serpents
that could swallow him whole.

The dugout bobbed gently and Tara's head sank on
his breast. What would his parents think? Likely that
he had run away — gone off to see the world as he had
so often said he someday would. He would not be
missed until nightfall, for Indian boys roamed about
pretty much as they pleased. The returning fishermen
had been too far away to see that he was merely a boy
alone on this great lake, and now they were all safely
on shore, hanging their nets up to dry, going in to
squat beside warm fires and eat *tortillas* and fresh
cooked fish.

"Hola, young nephew!" The words brought Tara
back from a dream world he was eager to forget.

"Lucio!" It was a joyful cry. "I wondered if anyone
would ever look for me on the lake."

"When I found the new dugout gone," Lucio said
with a slight edge to his voice, "I figured that someone
had stolen or borrowed it. Since my friends have boats
— and Tarascans do not steal — I figured that someone without a boat had borrowed it. I next thought
of you, my young rooster. But where is the paddle?"

"I lost it. It fell into the water." Tara's voice was shaky with remorse. What a way to treat his uncle.

Lucio leaned over and picked up something from the bottom of the dugout he was in. It was another spoon paddle, small enough for Tara to manage easily.

Lucio handed it over. "Hang on to this," he said. "I stayed up most of the night finishing it. That's why I was late this morning. There was a little smoothing still to do on the handle. And what do I find? That you've made off with my new dugout. I borrowed this one from José."

Tara flashed his uncle a grateful smile. How fortunate he was to have Lucio for his uncle-friend!

With a few deft splashes of his own paddle Lucio worked José's canoe around until the two flat ends of both dugouts were together.

"I'll push you to shore," Lucio said, "but you'll have to help. Use your paddle to guide the best you can."

Lucio was so strong and skillful that the two dugouts scooted across the water, and in no time at all Tara felt his canoe scrape bottom.

The women who were lined along the water's edge straightened up to see what new sort of boat this was, made in two parts. Tara laughed at the expression of surprise on the faces. They laughed back when they saw the canoe break in two and went back to their endless scrubbing of clothes against the rocks that edged the shore. The bushes alongside the lake were bright splashes of color from the garments hung there to dry.

Lucio pulled both dugouts well on shore and straightened up and stared down at Tara. "You will go no more on the lake without Lucio," he said sternly.

Tara shook his head. "I will go no more alone," he promised. "I am sorry that I lost your paddle."

"I'm glad that you did not lose the dugout and you in it." Lucio turned to stride away, throwing over his shoulder, "We will go to hunt the ducks tomorrow."

When Lucio came from the village the next morning, he held his hand behind his back until he was standing face to face with Tara. Lucio thrust out a long stick. "I made you one of your own," he said.

Tara gave a joyful cry as he accepted the gift — a hollow bamboo pole split down the middle, into which fitted a straight stick with a pronged fork at the end.

"I give you my thanks." Tara's voice was husky. How wonderful Lucio was to give him a fine *atl-atl* of his own. Tara balanced the lance in his hand and poised for throwing the spear as he had seen duck hunters do.

"Wait until we are out on the water, my anxious young rooster." Lucio chuckled slightly as he spoke. "Don't be in such a hurry. You rush headlong into every adventure."

They climbed into the dugout. Tara worked hard

with his smaller paddle and felt that he was doing a man-sized job helping his uncle. Suddenly Lucio stopped and held up a hand for silence. He pointed to a duck flying above.

"Don't move," Lucio whispered.

Tara held himself motionless.

Lucio dipped a paddle only now and then, silently and just hard enough to move the dugout slowly and smoothly.

A duck in front of the canoe disappeared under the water. "I will stab the first one," Lucio whispered. "See just how I hold the *atl-atl* to throw the pronged stick."

Scarcely had he finished the directions than the duck bobbed up from the water. Lucio's fork flew through the air. There was a short rustle of feathers. Lucio sped the canoe to where the duck floated and picked it up.

"I could never hit one," Tara cried. "Your hand darted as quick as the lightning. How could you know where to throw?"

"You may not hit the first duck — nor the tenth." Lucio chuckled. "But someday you will hit one, then you'll know how it's done. At any rate, here is a feast for your family tonight."

They traveled far on the lake that day, rounding the big bend of land where they were able to see the statue of José Morelos rising from the island.

Tara went out with Lucio for many days before he

finally was able to find his mark with the forked stick. By that time he was heartily tired of the calm surface of the lake — of squatting in a cramped dugout. Now he had decided that after all he did not wish to be a duck hunter or a fisherman when he grew up. The old dream of owning a burro that would carry him to far places to see the world was back with full force.

Off to Earn a Burro

ONE MORNING Tara picked up several *tortillas,* daubed them with a bean mixture which was on the back of the stone stove, and rolled them up. He put them in a cloth sack, thinking, Marina can tend the goats today.

"I am taking a journey," he said with a grin. Tara had decided that he would go to the great hacienda at the end of the dusty road. Don Ramón had a huge banana plantation and could certainly hire a boy for a few days so he could start earning pesos for a burro. And betweentimes he could stuff himself on bananas, warm and ripe from the trees.

Chalma was already at work on a large lacquer bowl. "You still long to see the world," he said in his mild tone. "It is well you have your adventures before the time comes when you must settle down to a man's work."

"You will take the gourd with the golden bird," Cheran said. Her tone was gentle as always, but there was that firmness in it which Tara was inclined to obey.

He knew that this gourd with the golden bird was a treasure which had been in the family since the beginning of time, so far as anyone could trace its origin. It was a small, perfectly formed vessel of lovely proportions. And upon its surface of black lacquer some master craftsman had long ago worked a breathtaking design of a bird traced in gold which had been rubbed deep into the grooves. Each other beautiful color had been rubbed in by hand, lovingly and with long labor. Then the unusual gourd had been passed down from generation to generation as an example of superb craftsmanship. It had come to be regarded as a good luck token and was always taken by the men of the family on any venture which might be dangerous.

It was bowl-shaped and could be used as a drinking vessel, or to carry a small amount of water, for tied to the neck it had a lid that fitted perfectly.

Tara laughed as his mother lifted the precious gourd from the cupboard and leaned to fill it with water from the large jar in the corner. "I am not going far, my dear mother," he said. "Nor will I run into terrible dangers. Best to leave the precious golden bird in its place until I do something really dangerous."

"You will not be in great danger today." She gave him a gentle half smile as she pressed the lid in place. "But I feel that you may need the good luck this golden bird will bring. And you will need water to drink, since you are taking food. Wear the golden bird under your shirt, for it is a treasure which might tempt thieves. Wear the blue serape, also. Now may good fortune go with you, my son."

"But the day is hot, my good mother. I do not need a serape."

"A sudden rain may come up. The evening may become chilly. Every wise man carries a serape." She lifted from the chest the blue blanket with the slit in the middle so that his head could be thrust through. It would serve as rain coat or cape, as needed.

She folded the serape until it was but a narrow width and placed it over one of his shoulders as the men of Mexico carried them. "You come from a family of famous weavers," she said. "Why should you go forth without a good serape?"

Tara stepped from the dim coolness of the adobe hut into the hot sun. His mother's ceremonious farewell made him feel like a daring adventurer as he set off on the trail with Tlaka at his heels. Strange,

Cheran always seemed to sense somehow what was in his mind.

The trail led through a jungle undergrowth. Tara climbed steadily until he came to the hilltop. Now for some distance the path would lead downhill or along level ground. Tara broke into a jogging run, thinking as he did so of the myth of the Tarascan runners of long ago who carried the catch of the lake to the palace of Montezuma and set it, still steaming hot, upon his table.

Tara had no idea how far the capital city was from the lake, but he was sure he would never be able to equal that feat, for within a short time his breath rasped in his throat. He ran until he could run no longer, then sank in the shade of a great tree. Tlaka sank panting beside him. After they had rested for a time, Tara drew the painted gourd from beneath his shirt and drank sparingly.

Pleadingly Tlaka looked at him. Tara found a shallow bowl-shaped rock and poured out a portion of water for the dog. Then they set out again.

The sun was past the middle of the sky when Tara reached the big hacienda. Everything was quiet about El Rancho. Tara guessed that it was siesta time. He seated himself beside the big gate and took out his sack of *tortillas,* which he divided with Tlaka.

A team of oxen stood dozing in a field, still hitched to the wooden yoke and plow. The peon who had evidently been driving them slept beneath a tree, his head pillowed on his serape, his sombrero over his face to discourage flies.

Several burros grazed by the side of the road. Tara looked them over critically and decided that he would buy the one with the glossy black coat and the black stripe down his spine. He was a strong-looking, handsome animal, and already Tara could imagine himself on the burro's back riding toward high adventure.

"What young waif are you?"

The words, added to a poke in the ribs, brought Tara upright from his pleasant dream world.

He leaped to his feet and stared up at a tall man wearing an enormous black sombrero. It took a moment for Tara to remember where he was.

"I — I came to work on El Rancho," he said. "I am a good worker. I must earn money to buy a burro. That one over there." He pointed to the black burro which already in his mind he owned.

The big man in the huge sombrero burst into laughter. "José, Lorenz, come!" he shouted.

Two Mexican men came up. "This boy wants to work on El Rancho," he said. "Says he must earn money to buy a burro."

Both men grinned.

José said, "He will be too old to ride a burro by the time he can earn enough pesos to buy one. Too young he is to do anything but herd goats."

"He wants Diablo over there." The man in the great sombrero broke into deep guffaws.

"Oh, that one!" And José also began to laugh.

"That one?" Lorenz made the remark sound like a question.

Tara was puzzled. What was so funny about a person's asking for work in order to buy himself a burro?

"I must have a burro," he explained with dignity, "because I have much traveling to do. I want to see the world."

The three Mexican men looked at each other and some message passed among them through their eyes.

"Do you own El Rancho?" Tara demanded of Big Sombrero.

The man puffed out his chest. "I do not own," he said. "But I am major domo. I am Big Boss."

"Then," Tara said stoutly, "I would like to work

for you. I can herd goats, but I would rather pick bananas, or something like that."

Big Sombrero put up a hand and stroked his chin while he stared at Tara. Now and then he chuckled and when he did, his two helpers also chuckled.

Tara felt his face grow hot, but he stood there, manfully erect.

"We have one goatherd," Big

Sombrero said, finally. "Maybe you could help drive burros loaded with bananas to the Big Market."

Tara's heart leaped. "I could do that," he said. "I will make you glad you hired me."

"You won't earn much," Big Sombrero said. "But it will be an adventure. I take it, that is what you want. And maybe — who knows — if you work well, you might be given the big black burro as your pay."

José gave a snort which sounded very like laughter, but when Tara looked at him, he seemed to be trying to recover from a coughing spell.

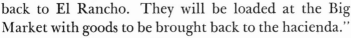

"You mean," Tara said slowly, so as to get the matter straight, "that if I work well in driving the banana train to market I will be given that fine burro as pay?"

"It could be." Big Sombrero nodded and Tara wondered about the twinkle in his eyes. "But of course you will be expected to help drive the loaded burros back to El Rancho. They will be loaded at the Big Market with goods to be brought back to the hacienda."

"Of course," Tara said.

"You will be here at this gate at sunup," Big Sombrero said.

"I will be here at sunup," Tara promised, noticing some men picking bananas in the orchard.

"May I help with the banana picking until evening?

My home is too far to go there and return by sunup. I would work just for enough bananas for my supper."

"José," Big Sombrero said, "take the boy and show him how to pick. Eat only ripe ones, boy, and don't get the bellyache. We'll need such a bright boy as you in the morning."

Chuckling, Big Sombrero strode off.

Diablo

4

THAT NIGHT Tara slept under a banana tree wrapped in his blue serape, with Tlaka snuggled against his back. Tara ate ripe bananas for supper and breakfast. The remaining *tortillas* he gave to his dog.

After being loaded with great baskets of bananas, the burros were driven through the wide gate. Big Sombrero stood by shouting orders.

Tara went to him and said, "I am ready to work, *señor.*"

"Take a long stick and help keep the burros going. Keep them in the road. Get busy now. Don't get in the way."

Tara searched about until he found a stick which would do to smack any stubborn burro on the rump.

"Get going! Go along!" he shouted in a big voice, running the length of the train.

A sleepy-looking fellow at the head of the train turned in surprise at the racket Tara was making.

"Slow down, young fellow," the sleepy man said. "You'll wear yourself out before you get started. It's a long, hot trip. Over mountains and dusty roads. Save some strength."

"Sí, señor." Tara grinned good-naturedly. He realized that he had been wasting good energy which burned up soon enough anyway under the hot sun. But he was terribly eager to please so that he would be paid the fine black burro.

To his delight he saw that Diablo was going along with the banana train, although, strangely enough, he carried no load.

One day Tara walked beside José. "Why does my friend there," Tara pointed to Diablo, "carry no load to market as the other burros do?"

José looked at the sleepy man and Tara saw him wink. "Diablo is too young to carry loads yet," he explained. "But no doubt by the time you get back to El Rancho, he will be strong enough to carry you."

"I hope so," Tara said. "He seems gentle enough. He lets me stroke his neck. I talk to him every day so that he will get used to me."

"It is wise to have him used to you," José said in a serious tone, although there was still a twinkle in his eyes.

Tara not only talked to Diablo. He told him what a special burro he was and the fine times they would have together when they went adventuring to see the world.

In time the black burro took to following him around like a dog.

"What a smart burro he is," Big Sombrero said. "He knows already that he is to belong to you."

Tara's heart gave a leap. Then he was doing his work well! Big Sombrero had said Diablo would be his. Perhaps the matter was already settled. From now on nearly every thought was about the black burro and the exciting times they would have together. There was scarcely room in his mind for any other thought.

The burro train passed through the village near Tara's home. He had known that it would, for there was no other route to the Big Market. He met Pepe in the village square.

"Will you go to my family," Tara asked in an important tone, "and tell them that I am helping to drive the burro train to the Big Market with bananas from El Rancho? I will be back some day, riding a fine black burro."

Pepe's eyes widened. "I will go with you!" he cried.

Big Sombrero astride a fine burro rode up just then. "You will not go," he said. "One boy is worth half a man; two boys are worth no boy at all. And send your dog with your friend, boy. He's a nuisance."

So Tara hustled off with the train while Pepe held Tlaka. It would have been nice to have Pepe and Tlaka along for company. But the important thing was to please Big Sombrero so that he, Tara, would earn the black burro.

The journey was long and tiring, but at last the Big Market was reached and then Tara forgot his weariness in staring at the many sights. They drove straight to the *zocolo,* or big square, where the owner of the hacienda met the train and made arrangements for trading the bananas. They were taken off the backs of the burros and straightway various packages and bundles were loaded onto the burros. The journey commenced back to El Rancho without Tara's having had much time to look around. But never had he seen or imagined such fine large buildings, such stores of merchandise as were displayed around the square. And such a steady stream of fine shiny automobiles streamed past that he wondered if all of the *americanos* to the north were coming to Mexico.

He was not too disappointed that he had not had more time to wander around and see the sights of the Big Market city, for soon he would own Diablo and then they could roam the whole world and see everything there was to see everywhere.

When the train got back to El Rancho the owner was already there. He had traveled in a big shiny car which went as fast as the wind. He was standing beside the gate when the burro train was driven through. A fine lady was standing beside him. Tara decided that she must be the *señora* of the hacienda.

Tara helped with the unloading of the burros and then lent a hand in driving them out into a pasture.

He heard the owner say, "That Diablo! I see he's

still with the herd. You haven't found out a way to outsmart him yet, eh, José?"

"*Sí, señor,*" José said. "Overseer promised him to the boy over there for helping to drive the herd to the Big Market."

The owner laughed. "Overseer is smart," he said. "He hires help for me cheap."

Tara was puzzled by this remark, but it appeared that the hacienda owner had no objection to his having the black burro. He had feared something might happen to keep his dream from coming true. Being parched with thirst, he went to the well to wait his turn for a drink. When the others had drunk he pulled his gourd from under his shirt and filled it with cool water.

"Juan," he heard the fine lady say. "Do you see the gourd that boy has? It is a real *tecomate.* Bring it here, boy."

Tara did as he was bidden, but his heart fluttered when she took it from his hands.

"Juan!" she said, turning the gourd over and over in her slim hands. "Just see this fine piece of work. There is nothing so fine in the museum. It is genuine Tarascan. And very old. The finest I have ever seen. See how perfectly the lid fits. The workmanship is exquisite. I must have it."

She turned upon Tara. "Where did you get this?" she said sharply.

"It has been in my family always," he said, rather

resenting her tone. It was as though she suspected him of stealing it.

"The boy may be telling the truth," the man said. "Many Tarascan families — other tribes, too, pass these treasures from generation to generation."

"But he shouldn't be carrying it around with him."

"My mother made me carry it to bring me good luck," Tara explained.

The lady's fingers tightened on the *tecomate*. "I must have this, Juan," she insisted.

"How much will you take for it?" the man asked.

"I would not sell it." Tara reached out and would have taken the gourd from the lady but she jerked her hands away.

"Bargain with him. I must have this." A shrill note had come into her voice.

"You said you wanted a burro, I believe," the man said. "You may take your pick of the burros on the place in exchange for this little bowl of yours."

"But I was already promised the black burro!" The words came out in a wail of protest. "I would not exchange my *tecomate* for all of the burros on El Rancho — or in all of Mexico. That golden bird is a treasure that must remain in our family forever."

The argument went on for some time, with the fine lady demanding the *tecomate*, the man growing cross with Tara, but Tara remaining firm in his stand.

Finally Juan threw up his hands in despair. "There's no use," he said. "The boy is stubborn as a burro. You know how these Indians are. Especially the Tarascans. They do hand these things from generation to generation and they come to consider them good luck charms. They believe that evil would come to them if they parted with such a treasure."

He turned to Tara. "All right boy. A bargain is a bargain. Go put a bridle on the black burro and ride him away. He's all yours."

"I give you my thanks," Tara said. He held out his hand for the precious gourd with the golden bird. The fine lady unwillingly let him take it.

José went to the stable with him and gave him a rope bridle and then went with him to the pasture. Diablo came at Tara's whistle, as he had learned to do on the journey back from the Big Market.

He and José had no difficulty in slipping the bridle over the burro's head. Tara stroked the shaggy black neck and talked soothingly to Diablo before he threw himself onto his back.

In no time at all, Tara found himself plunk on the ground with Diablo almost sitting in his lap. He picked himself up, not hurt much, except by the roar of laughter which arose from the El Rancho workmen, who had gathered around in a circle

"A fine way to treat me!" Tara sputtered into Diablo's ear.

Then Diablo raised his head and a great *he-haw* came from his mouth, as though he were echoing the laughter of the men.

Tara took a firmer grip on the bridle rein and again climbed onto the burro's back.

Again Diablo sat down and Tara slid to the ground. And again the El Rancho workers roared with laughter.

Once more Tara tried to ride. Again Diablo sat down and Tara bumped to the ground.

Angrily he turned to stalk from the ranch down the trail toward home.

Diablo was right at his heels.

"You wanted a burro. You've got a burro," he heard José's taunting voice shout at him. And once more that maddening laughter of the workers followed him.

A Wish Gone Wrong

5

Diablo followed Tara along the shady trail leading to his home. He had a burro all right. But what a burro!

Diablo nudged at his shoulder, pushing him playfully. At times, though, he ran ahead, kicking up his heels.

"You're a lively one, you are," Tara said. "But I can't see what good you'll be to me. You act more like a dog than a burro. And I have a dog that suits me. You've spoiled everything for me. That's what you have."

Diablo threw back his head, drew back his upper lip, and let out a blasting *he-haw*. From time to time he let out another of these blasts, which echoed from hill to hill like giant's laughter.

It was one of these he-haws close to Tara's home which drew his family out of their adobes. Everyone looked at Tara in amazement as he walked along with the black burro trotting at his heels. Tara threw back his shoulders and tried to look jaunty about the whole thing, but he was cringing inside from what he knew was in store.

"What a fine burro!" his father cried. "Just what we need. When we go to the Great City, if we go, he can carry a large load of our wares to the market place."

"Are we going to the Great City?" Tara cried in surprise. "When do we go?"

"I said IF we go," Chalma replied. "And I had not planned to take you. But perhaps I will need you to drive this fine burro."

"He has not been trained to work yet. . . ." Tara's voice trailed off. "He will not let me ride yet."

The Wise One spoke up, "Chalma will take care of that. He knows about training burros. You are too young. Your voice has not the ring of authority."

Zolic, Kalli the grandmother, Cheran, Marina, with Chiqua the little one dangling in her *rebozo* — all stood in a circle staring at Diablo.

Even the dog Tlaka came up and sniffed at Diablo's heels. The burro lowered his head and Tara thought he was going to nip Tlaka, but the two animals put noses together and held them that way for a long moment. Tara sensed in an instant they were friends.

Chalma stepped forward and took hold of the rope bridle. "Climb on his back," he said. "It is time your animal was learning that you're his master."

Tara, though, hung back. "I'm hungry," he said. "I smell warm *tortillas* and red beans."

"Now!" his father insisted. "The food will wait. Take a short ride, then we will hobble the burro so he will not stray until he becomes used to his new home."

Tara took hold of the mane and eased himself onto Diablo's back. Diablo promptly sat down and Tara slid to the ground. Diablo raised his head and out came that great *he-haw*. Tara looked up, waiting for his family's laughter. But no one laughed. Everyone seemed shocked.

Chalma jerked on the bridle and the burro stood up.

"Try again," Chalma said.

"It's no use. He does that every time." Tara was thoroughly miserable.

"Why did you bring such an animal home?" Zolic said. "He will eat the food our faithful burro needs."

"I could not help it. He followed me. He follows me just like a dog. I wanted a burro I could ride. I worked hard on the drive to take the bananas from El Rancho to the Big Market. I was promised a burro. And this is what I got. He tags at my heels all the time. I can't get rid of him."

"We could not even sell such an animal," his mother said. "We can't afford to feed him. What shall we do?"

"Maybe you can take him far away and lose him," Marina suggested.

"How can I lose him if he follows me every place?" Tara said crossly. "Now I'm really hungry and I'm going to eat."

He went into the adobe where the cooking was done. Diablo would have followed him into the room had not all of them seized switches and chased him away.

"Go back to El Rancho, you black devil," Tara shouted. "I don't want you. You make me madder than I ever was before. I had hoped for so much from my burro. But you make everyone laugh at me."

Diablo blasted out one of his he-haws but this time there was a pathetic note to it; it did not sound like laughter.

"I'm sorry," Tara said. "I do like you. But you know very well my father will not let me keep you unless you earn your keep."

At that, Diablo turned and kicked up his heels. Going to the edge of the clearing, he started cropping the meager grass which was scarce enough for Toto.

Tara carefully folded the blue serape and placed it in the chest. He took the gourd with the golden bird from under his shirt and handed it to his mother. "A fine *señora* tried to buy this from me," he said. "I had trouble getting it from her hands. Her fingers fastened around it like claws."

"Anyone would like to buy this," Cheran said, holding the lovely *tecomate* carefully. "But it is not for sale. It is our treasure. The golden bird brings us good luck."

The next day Tara went down to the lake to seek out Lucio. Of course both Tlaka and Diablo followed at his heels. As he went through the village Pepe and the other youngsters ran out, crying, "You have a fine burro, Tara. Why aren't you riding him?"

"He's too young," Tara said crossly. He wished they would leave him alone.

"He looks big and strong," Pepe insisted.

Tara started to run. Diablo kicked up his heels and ran too. Pepe ran right along beside Tara. Gradually the other boys and girls dropped behind, but Pepe stayed.

"I have business with Lucio," Tara said.

It was impossible to hurt Pepe's feelings, though. He only grinned and tagged right along.

Tara found Lucio sitting in front of his adobe
mending a net.

"Ho, there, my young rooster!" he exclaimed looking up. "So you finally got your wish. A fine burro."

"I got a burro. But what a burro!" Tara bit off
the words.

"What's the matter with him?"

Tara wished that Pepe were far away, but there
was nothing to do but let him witness his shame. He
took hold of Diablo's mane and climbed on his back.
Diablo sat down and blasted out his maddening
he-haw.

Pepe threw back his head and laughed and laughed
until he had to double up and hold his sides.

Even Lucio had to chuckle. "I see your burro has a bad habit," he remarked.

"And what a bad habit! He's no good. My father won't let me keep a burro who won't work. He'll eat the grass the good burro needs."

Lucio nodded. "We'll have to figure out something," he said. "Will he carry burdens — other than people?"

"I don't know. I suppose not. He didn't carry any bananas to market or anything else going back to El Rancho."

Lucio rose and gathered up an armload of the big nets which had been spread to dry. He made a bundle of them. They were bulky but light in weight. He placed them on Diablo's back. Diablo sat down, but this time he did not laugh.

Lucio picked up the nets and rolled them up. Then he stood staring at the black burro and scratching his head. Tara, watching him, began to lose heart. He had thought his uncle so smart that he could find an answer to any problem, but it was plain he didn't know what to do about Diablo. Even the Wise One, whom everyone in the village consulted, had not known what to do about the black burro who sat down.

"I can't even get rid of him," Tara wailed. "He follows me just like Tlaka does."

"Let's go fishing," Lucio suggested. "I can figure things out best when I'm on the water. Sorry, Pepe, the dugout won't hold more than two of us. Why don't you stay here and try to chase the burro away. Maybe if Tara isn't around, he'll decide to go back to El Rancho, where there's lots of grass."

Tara brightened. Lucio did have good ideas.

Pepe also liked the idea. "I'll get the other boys to help me," he said. "They'll help me drive the black burro away."

"Don't hurt him, though," Tara said with a worried frown as he stepped into the dugout. After all, he liked the black burro even if he proved to be a problem rather than a joy.

When he and Lucio returned late in the afternoon the shore was deserted. There was no Pepe and no Diablo. Even Tlaka was gone.

But when Tara got back to his adobe, there was Diablo right in the middle of the yard, acting as though he owned the place. Tara groaned. After giving his mother the string of whitefish he had brought, he told Chalma and Zolic about Lucio's plan to get rid of Diablo. A plan that had not worked.

"You'll have to get rid of him," Chalma said. "He eats his head off."

"He even ate some of my purple wisteria," his mother wailed. "I beat him off with my broom and he laughed at me."

"He is a black devil," Zolic said. "It was an evil day when you brought him home."

Tara swallowed hard. He picked up one of the

whitefish his mother was cooking, rolled it in a warm *tortilla,* and stuffed them into his mouth. Why had everything worked out so badly? He had wished with all his might for a burro of his own. He had got his wish all right.

A Useful Friend

6

Tara ran toward the lake. He skirted the village, for he wanted to avoid Pepe and the other boys. Of course Diablo was right at his heels, as was Tlaka. Tara was sure that Pepe had told all of the boys and girls of the village about his burro who sat down and would not be ridden. And he was sure that the minute they saw him every last one of them would burst out laughing.

He went to Lucio's adobe, taking a long way around. But Lucio was gone. Tara hurried to the edge of the lake. Lucio was just pushing off in his boat, his net poised like gossamer dragonfly wings.

When Tara shouted to him, Lucio started back to shore.

"What now, young rooster?" he called out.

Tara pointed wordlessly but dramatically at Diablo, now standing with his head resting on his owner's shoulder.

"Friendly creature, isn't he?" Lucio grinned. "I never saw such a burro."

"I'm sure he thinks he's a person," Tara said as Lucio grounded his dugout and stepped ashore. "He doesn't act like a burro."

"He certainly doesn't." Lucio agreed. "He didn't chase away very well, did he?"

Tara shook his head. "I haven't seen Pepe to find out what happened. I don't want to see him because he laughs at me on account of Diablo."

Lucio nodded understandingly. "We'll have to figure out something else."

He stood for a long while, staring at the burro and stroking his chin. While this was going on Diablo remained with his chin resting on Tara's shoulder, a blissful, sleepy expression on his face.

"Come with me," Lucio finally said. With his nets over his shoulder he strode toward his adobe. Tara and his animals followed.

Lucio went into the house and shortly came out with some pieces of leather and rope. He went a short distance on a side hill and came back with two round very prickly cacti. He then rigged up a sort of harness. Passing it under Diablo's tail, he tied the ropes together over his rump.

"Now get on," Lucio said. "But be ready to hang on tight."

Tara grasped Diablo firmly around the neck. He felt himself sliding as Diablo sat down, but suddenly, with a snort, the burro was up. His heels lashed out three times, then he stood still.

"It worked." Lucio chuckled. "Now kick his ribs with your heels. Make him go."

Tara did so and Diablo stepped meekly forward.

"Stop!" Lucio said, taking firm hold of the bridle. "Now slide off and try it again."

Tara slid off then mounted again. Diablo tried to sit down, but quickly jerked up to his four feet. And Lucio led him forward while Tara kicked his ribs.

Time after time this routine was repeated. Finally Lucio gently removed the harness containing the cacti that had jabbed into Diablo's backside whenever he sat down. Perhaps the burro did not know that the

painful contraption had been removed. At any rate,
he walked forward as a well-behaved burro should.

Lucio rolled up the harness with the burs inside.
"Use this whenever Diablo feels like sitting," he said.
"I don't think you'll have much more trouble with
him. He's smart. He learns fast. You've got yourself
a good and useful friend there."

"Thank you! Thank you!" Tara called gratefully.
"No one ever had such a friend as you."

Proudly he rode through the village. Pepe was
there playing marbles with a group of boys. They all
stared goggle-eyed at Tara as he rode past them with
a wave of the hand. No one laughed now.

He was prouder than ever when he rode into the
yard surrounded by the adobe houses where his family
lived and worked.

"Come and see me!" he shouted.

Faces popped along the doorways and in a moment
everyone was crowding around.

"You can ride him!" Marina cried. "Let me ride,
Tara, please."

"Not until he is better trained," Tara said in an
important manner.

"A fine burro! A very fine burro!" his father said.
It was plain that he was pleased that Diablo had
decided to become a useful member of the family.

After this day Diablo now and then decided to try
his sitting down trick, but every time he did so, Tara
brought out the cactus harness and quickly put a stop

to such foolishness. Now Tara was the envy of all the boys of the village for none of them had so fine a burro.

Diablo carried loads of wood and dried grass. He carried serapes and *rebozos* to market to trade for things other people made.

And betweentimes Tara rode him in every direction, starting out early in the morning with a sack of *tortillas* and a gourd of water and returning late at night. He was seeing the world all around his home. Now he was yearning to see more distant points.

"What is it you are searching for, Restless One?" Lucio asked him one day when he stopped in to visit his uncle.

"I don't know," Tara admitted. "Something. I don't know what yet. But when I find it, I will know."

Lucio nodded.

"You used to feel the same way; you told me so," Tara reminded him. "You wanted a bicycle so you could see the world. You were looking for something. Did you ever find it?"

For a long moment Lucio was silent, then he said, "I think I did. But I had to come back here to find it."

"What was it?"

Lucio shrugged. "Contentment, I think. Yes, that must have been it. I was always restless as you are when I was your age. I wandered far and wide, looking for something. I didn't find it in the Great City, although there is everything one would hope to see.

But what I was looking for can't be seen. It must be felt."

Tara was disappointed. He had only a vague idea of what contentment was. But he knew it wasn't the thing he was looking for — whatever it was was pushing him, pulling him. He must search for it, and soon. But when he saw it, he would recognize it. Of that he was very sure.

Lucio Steals a Bride

For some time Tara had been aware of a change in Lucio. His uncle still took him on the lake to fish or shoot ducks, and he was as proud of Diablo as Tara himself was.

"I never saw a smarter burro," Lucio often said.

Now Tara always rode Diablo to the lakeshore. Whenever Tara went out in the canoe Tlaka and Diablo stood watching as he paddled away. Both animals always held a hurt look in their eyes, as though they wanted to be taken along. It made Tara feel sorry that he had to leave them, although he did not have to worry about Diablo. Pepe and other boys tried to ride him, but he always sat down and let them slide to the hard ground with a bump. They did not know about Lucio's clever trick with the cactus harness, and Tara certainly wasn't going to tell them. Diablo also had another habit. Pepe told Tara that he had seen three different men try to lead Diablo away, but the burro bared his teeth and nipped them and sent them running. Aye! This Diablo was a clever one.

The difference in Lucio was something Tara could not quite explain. Certainly his uncle was as kind and friendly as ever. But his mind was on something else. When fishing, his eyes often held a faraway look. And in shooting ducks he was not as quick as usual and often missed his throw.

But before long Tara's mind was on other things too, for soon it would be time for the main fiesta of the Tarascans. The fiesta would last for three days, during which time ceremonies would be held to bring good crops for the coming year.

This was the children's favorite celebration of the many throughout the year, because they could take an active part in it. One of the activities would be the mock market during which adults and youngsters would parade around the square displaying tiny copies of the things they made to earn a living. House builders carried small houses. Bakers made loaves an inch long. Weavers made doll-sized blankets. Even *tortillas* were no bigger than coins.

The afternoon before the fiesta, Tara and his family went to the giant olive trees outside the village. Marina and Tara laughingly placed on their backs the small crates containing tiny serapes and painted gourds that they had made themselves. They bent over and groaned as though the loads were almost more than they could carry. The parents, too, carried small crates with tiny wares. Zolic and the grandmother rode the two burros, and behind them were carried the rolled grass mats on which all of them would sleep during the nights of the fiesta.

There would not be much sleeping, for the ancient olive grove was crowded and everyone was in a fiesta mood. Food was cooked on braziers, and much trading was done. The smell of smoke and of *tortillas,* beans, chile, and fish hung heavy on the air and made Tara feel quite famished, until he had eaten well with his own family and several groups of friends.

There was visiting, and the band played and people danced. The women and girls were dressed in bright full skirts and gaily embroidered blouses with *rebozos* draped gracefully over their shoulders. They danced in rows, rather primly and with modest eyes downcast. The men, in their clean white cotton suits, were very nimble with their feet — especially Lucio, whose sandals slapped the hard earth so fast that Tara could hardly follow them with his eyes. Finally Lucio picked up a gourd, stepped to the fountain to fill it with water, then placed it on his head and danced and whirled and kicked his feet in a lively fashion without spilling a drop. Aye, a remarkable fellow was his uncle, Tara thought proudly, but he saw his uncle's eyes too much on the face of a certain girl. Something strange happened to Tara's stomach when he saw Lucio look so often at this girl. He wondered if he had eaten something which disagreed with him. Finally he went off to find his sleeping mat beside the grandparents who had long ago sought theirs.

The next morning the band blared and the people got in line to march into the village. The burro drivers led the way, with sacks stuffed with straw to represent merchandise. They were followed by the crate carriers. Tara was proud to be driving the handsomest burro of all. Diablo showed off well by stepping high and now and then rolling back his lips to show his teeth and grin. Everyone noticed them.

Then came the plows drawn by oxen, with the wooden share of the plow hooked over the yoke and the beam dragging just as though the drivers were plowing the field. The heads and horns of these oxen were decorated with flowers, bright streamers of paper and corn husks, as well as small corn cakes shaped like animals.

Last in the procession came the children, carrying tiny crates on their backs, filled with small wares. When they reached the village square the burro drivers unloaded their mock wares while several actors pretended to plow a small plot where already there was a tiny cornfield with green stalks growing. One of the men wore a great white cape, a wooden mask, and carried a gun. He was supposed to be the watchman of the cornfield. At one end of the cornfield were a stuffed fox and opossum. The watchman stalked about and finally spied the animals. He hurriedly loaded his gun and fired, then ran and picked up the animals he had just "shot." The children all shrieked

with glee, although they had seen this same performance many times.

A woman and girl followed the plow and pretended
to plant corn. Then the band began to play and the
women and girls danced around the cornfield. Tara,
looking at Marina, was surprised by the change in her.
For once she did not carry Chiqua wrapped in her
rebozo. The little one had been left with the grandmother. Marina's feet were flying and so was her dark
hair. Her eyes were sparkling and her lips were parted
in a happy smile. Why, she was pretty. Prettier than
any of the other girls. Usually she was busy baby
tending or patting *tortillas,* but now she was like any
other young girl having a good time.

In the afternoon the mock market was held. People
picked up their small crates and paraded around the
plaza, trying to outshout each other with, "Come
quickly, everyone. Look at what I have. Buy it before
it is gone."

"How much?" Pepe with a wide grin pointed to
one of the small painted gourds carried in Tara's crate.

"Five hundred pesos," Tara said soberly.

"I buy," Pepe said, extending a stick of chewing
gum.

Solemnly Tara handed over the gourd and accepted
Pepe's payment.

When all the wares were sold, the band played in
the center of the plaza. While the old people sat on
the benches and the children romped, the young men

and girls paraded. The girls, arm in arm, going in one direction, pretending not to know the young men were there; the young men going in the other direction, laughing and jabbing each other with their elbows.

Tara was a bit disgusted to see Lucio acting in this manner. It seemed undignified. And to make matters worse, Lucio carried a large rose in his hand which he waved in front of his face in the most silly manner. What had happened to his hero uncle? Tara wondered.

He was about to turn away when he saw Lucio boldly pass the rose to the girl he had been watching when he danced so briskly the night before. The girl accepted the flower without giving Lucio more than a fleeting glance from her large, dark eyes. Once again Tara sought out his sleeping mat, feeling rather sick and cold.

The next two days were spent feasting and observing the rituals for a plentiful year ahead. Saturday night was the end of the fiesta.

Sunday morning the weary people in the olive grove gathered up their grass mats and their cooking things and soon the crowd thinned out. As Tara was tying the mats on to Diablo's back Lucio came striding between the trees and drew Tara off to one side.

"I have a secret. A big secret," he whispered. "I want you to be before the steps of the cathedral when church lets out."

"Why?" Already a chill was around Tara's heart.

"I am going to steal Erendia. I want you there."

"Steal Erendia!" The words came out like a wail.

"Ssh!" Lucio put his hand over Tara's mouth. "Would you shout my secret to the world? Spoil my plan?"

Tara gulped and said nothing. He knew what this meant and it seemed that his world had suddenly grown bleak and chilly. It was the Tarascan custom for a young man to "steal" the girl he wanted for his bride, although the theft was done with her permission. This, then, was the reason for the change in Lucio. This girl Erendia had come between them. Things could never be the same again. How he hated Erendia!

The smile faded from Lucio's handsome face as he saw Tara's expression. He must have sensed what was going on in the boy's mind, for he stooped down and put his hands on Tara's shoulders.

"Things will be the same with us," he said soberly. "You will always be my friend. That is why I want you there — this most important day of my life. I will still be the same Lucio — your uncle. We will still go fishing and duck shooting. But when a young man gets to be my age, he longs for a wife to tend his home fire — to cook his *tortillas*. You will understand how it is when you are older. Now cheer up. I want you to come to my wedding."

He stood up and squeezed Tara's shoulder and once again warmth flooded into the boy's heart. In spite of Erendia, things — boy-to-man things — would be the

same as ever. Of course no mere girl could do the
things with Lucio that they had done together. How
foolish he had been to dislike this girl. She had not
come between them.

Tara was at the steps of the cathedral when the
people came out, but Lucio was nowhere to be seen.
Erendia came down the steps surrounded by two
women and two girls. She was laughing and chattering
nervously. Her eyes darted here and there among
those who lounged about the square. Then there was
a sudden commotion. Lucio darted from behind a
huge tree and dashed up the steps, seized the screaming
Erendia, and threw her over his shoulder.

She struggled and called for help, but Tara knew
that she was willing — that the details of this theft
had been arranged by her and Lucio according to
the Tarascan custom. The women and girls who were
with her likewise screamed for help. From then on
it was a game into which Tara, Pepe, and others leaped
happily. If the men of Erendia's family caught Lucio,
the girl would be taken back to her parent's home
and the whole thing would have to be done again.
Besides, failure would bring disgrace to Lucio — make
him lose face. So Tara urged Pepe and all of their
friends to help keep Erendia's men folks from reaching
Lucio. His handsome young uncle with his bride
over his shoulder was able to reach his dugout. He
carefully seated Erendia in the canoe, shoved off, and

leaped in. Lucio paddled rapidly until he was upon the deep waters, then he yelled with triumph and waved his lollipop paddle. Erendia also waved and looked very happy about having been stolen.

Lucio looked especially handsome in his pleated white shirt and bright red sash above his white cotton trousers. Erendia looked like a flower in her gaily embroidered blouse and bright blue skirt with many pleats in back. Over her head and draped across one shoulder she wore a *rebozo* of many colors.

Knowing what to expect, Tara joined with the members of Lucio's family. According to the custom they carried gifts to the "stolen" girl's family, to make up to them for the loss of their daughter. It was according to the custom, too, that the women of Erendia's family should weep and the men rage, for never had parents had a more wonderful daughter, they shouted. But as the gifts piled up within their door, their grief died down, and before long everyone was enjoying a feast.

Later in the day Erendia's parents would carry gifts to Lucio's house, to show that they had forgiven him for stealing Erendia and that he was now a welcome member of the family.

No doubt Lucio and Erendia were already in the town around the bend of the lake, where they both signed their names in a large ledger. The clerk would then pronounce them married according to the civil law of Mexico. Late in the afternoon they would return to their own village and together climb the steps of the cathedral. Within its holy, candlelighted interior they would recite the religious marriage vows.

Tara had almost given up waiting, when at last he saw Lucio's canoe coming slowly across the lake. There were not many people around when the bride and groom came ashore and went into the cathedral. But the news spread fast and there was a crowd waiting when the twice-married couple came down the cathedral steps.

Wreaths of flowers were thrown around the necks of both, and nearly everyone else wore garlands of flowers. Now Erendia was sparkling and gay and broke into a song and danced along the path, her full skirts whirling. Lucio sang, also, and took Erendia's hand and danced all the way to his adobe.

Soon Erendia and her women relatives were busy making *atole,* a corn gruel, which would serve as food and drink to the many guests. The singing and dancing went on in the cramped hot room. Tara went outside, where he met Pepe. Together they strolled toward the lake and amused themselves by skimming rocks across the water.

When Tara became aware that a silence had fallen upon the merrymakers in the small adobe, he hurried to the doorway to observe the third part of the marriage ceremony. Those inside the house were crowded against the walls. Erendia was standing surrounded by her own people. Now she left them and walked slowly

toward Lucio's people, who were grouped together.
She sank to the ground before Lucio's father, leaned
forward, and kissed his bare feet. This performance
she repeated before her mother-in-law and the other
relatives.

When she had abased herself before all of her in-
laws, Lucio went through the same performance before Erendia's family. This last ceremony united the
couple according to the tribal custom.

Tara heaved a big sigh. Erendia had gone back to
brewing *atole*, and once again the guests were shouting, singing, and dancing. He knew that this would

continue until dawn, but he was weary and longed for his own sleeping mat in the quiet adobe high on the mountainside.

Where was Diablo? He whistled several times before he felt Diablo's hard chin resting on his shoulder.

"Good old Diablo!" Tara said as he put his arms about the hairy neck. "Carry me home, my friend."

He heard Tlaka sniffing and panting at the burro's heels as he rode slowly homeward. He thought of the wedding and again the strange, sick feeling swept through him. Would things ever be quite the same with him and Lucio? he wondered.

Time of the Evil Eye

For a time after the wedding Tara was not able to go to the lake to see if things were still the same between him and Lucio. In fact, his wanderings were over for a while, because it was the time for planting and everyone but the grandparents worked long hours in the cornfield and the garden where squashes, melons, and beans were planted. It was always the busiest season of the year; the ground had to be cleared and made ready and the seeds planted before the good rains came.

Every year at this season a man came from the other side of the village with his ox and turned over the ground with his wooden plow. For this service Chalma had to work several days in the field of the man who owned the ox. But this year, before Chalma sent for the plowman he looked Diablo over for a long time and stroked his chin. Then he rubbed his hand over the mule's smooth flank.

"Your burro has grown much, Tara," he said. "He is almost as large as a small ox. He looks strong. . . . "

Tara quickly put an arm about Diablo's neck. He knew what was in his father's mind and he had no wish to turn his friend into a work beast.

As though in answer to what Tara was thinking, Chalma went on. "After all, every member of the family works hard so that all of us can live and eat. It hardly seems fair that the strongest one of us should eat his head off to be kept mainly as a pleasure pet."

"But Diablo does work hard," Tara burst out in defense. "He carried giant loads of wood from the mountains, and great loads of feed."

Chalma nodded. "He works well — when there is work to be done. But there is not enough for him to do to keep him from growing so fat that your legs stick out at the sides when you ride him."

Tara chuckled at his father's little joke. Diablo was plump, but not that fat.

"We will try him with a plow tomorrow," Chalma said in a manner which told Tara that the matter was settled.

So early the next morning Chalma led Diablo to the flattest part of ground against the hillside, and with a rope tied a wooden plow to him.

"Go on! Go on!" Chalma cried slapping Diablo with the rope and pushing on the plow to give him the idea. Diablo looked back over his shoulder to see what was going on. Then he gave several little kicks with his heels and bent his head to look for stray bits of grass.

Chalma took the end of the rope, which was knotted, and hit Diablo a smart smack with it. Diablo looked around and rolled back his upper lip and grinned at Chalma, who was growing angrier by the minute.

Tara stepped up to Diablo and put an arm about the burro's neck and whispered in his ear, "Do not anger my father, my friend. We must all work, if we want to eat. It is the way of life. So, bend your head. Pull the plow. The work will be over in a few days. Then after the seeds are in, we will roam the hills and valleys again. We will see more of the world."

As Tara dropped his arm, Diablo put his chin on his master's shoulder for a moment and closed his eyes with that silly, sleepy expression he wore at such times. Tara was afraid that Diablo was about to be stubborn again, but in a moment he raised his head, then leaned forward on the rope, and the plow began to move. The dusty earth rolled back behind it.

"That rascal understands every word I say to him," Tara shouted as his father flashed him a happy smile. "He is the most wonderful burro in the world."

Diablo did the work in less time than a plodding ox would have taken, and Chalma now would not have to repay the plowman for his time.

Chalma, Cheran, Tara, and Marina all trudged along the rows with sacks of seeds on their backs and sticks in their hands, dropping the seeds into holes they made as they went along, then quickly smoothing over the planted places with their sticks. It was backbreaking, wearying work, but it had to be done if they were to eat.

At last it was finished. The seeds were in the ground. Soon the rains would come and the seeds

would spring up into green plants and finally produce good and nourishing food. Every year of his life Tara had seen the good earth produce this miracle. He thought it was something that would never fail.

This year, though, it was not the same. Moon followed moon and the rains did not come to the lake district. The blazing sun beat down day after day drying the earth. A layer of dust lay over the trees and shrubs.

The corn, if it came up at all, was scanty and with kernels poorly filled out. The few squashes and melons were small and dry. The grain crops failed. To make matters worse, even the fish of the lake were harder to catch, and the ducks had long ago disappeared.

Later in the season scarcely a day passed when the gaunt villagers or farmers did not come to the abode of Zolic the Wise One to ask what they should do.

Zolic had a ready answer for those who came asking his advice. "It is because you have departed from the ways of your fathers," he said sternly. "The old ways are best. Plant the crops when the moon is right for planting. Cultivate them with our good wooden tools which do not tear deep into the Earth Mother as do the metal tools of the *americanos*. Earn your livelihoods by keeping up the fine craftsmanship of your fathers and mothers. Those arts are being lost — cheapened because you are greedy for the pesos of the white tourists. You are losing your craftsmanship. Who then will pass it on to the young? For generations we have made those things which have provided usefulness and beauty and joy for our lives. One man makes what another man needs. The other man makes what I need. We trade our wares, and everyone has enough. It is better than begging or becoming slaves to the rich."

Tara had heard these words of his grandfather so many times that he knew them by heart. When he was younger he had believed them, but lately he was beginning to wonder whether this explained their present hardships. Why should the fact that many of their people were changing over from the old way to the new cause the rains to stay away — the crops to fail? If it was punishment from above, it seemed to him unjust and severe. The whole thing was very puzzling.

No one had enough to eat. The dwindling supply of precious corn and beans must be stretched. Hunger was the daily lot of everyone.

His mother's face was becoming sharp and thin. Chiqua the little one cried night and day and now her head bobbed on her neck from weakness. Then in a few days her small body was put in a box and laid in the ground beside the others in the City of the Dead. Her toys and a painted gourd of water were placed beside her. The neighbors brought bread made in the shape of animals, and candles were burned on her grave and the graves of the other children of the family buried there.

The band played and girls and children danced while the little coffin was being covered with dirt. It was unseemly to show grief because it would make the departed one sad, so a sort of celebration was made of the burial of children. They had not had time to enjoy fiestas, and the lack must be made up to them.

Cheran, however, was unable to conceal her grief. She held up both hands, the fingers outspread on one and the forefinger of the other sticking up. "So many as these fingers I have laid away in the City of the Dead."

She sobbed and covered her face with her *rebozo,* turning away from where they were making a mound over the coffin.

Chalma put an arm over her shoulder and led her away. Tara followed.

"Soon there will be another little one," Chalma said.

She would not be comforted. "Why? Why? Why." She sobbed. "Why are so many born only to die? They are so soft and helpless — "

"Ssh!" Chalma whispered. "Such words may offend the Great Power. Someone has put the Ojo — the Evil Eye — upon this little one, as upon the others."

Slow hot weeks dragged by. All color seemed faded from the cloudless sky. The earth grew parched and thirsty and the brassy sun blazed without mercy. The rains did not come and did not come and hunger increased among the Tarascan people.

Zolic called his family together one evening beneath the camelina, which had its roots sunk so deep into the heart of the earth that the drought could not wither its beauty. Solemnly they discussed the trouble that had fallen over the land. Something must be done to ease the hunger of themselves and their neighbors.

Everyone, even Tara and Marina, was called upon to speak whatever thoughts were in his or her mind regarding the problem. Then, when everyone had spoken, Zolic sat in long silence. It would be his decision as to what should be done.

At last he spoke. "Chalma, Cheran, Tara. You will journey to the Great City. Take along the best of our wares — the lacquer, the serapes, the *rebozos* to sell at the big market where many rich people come. Then you will turn the money you get into food to bring back to our people."

Wild excitement raced through Tara's heart. At last he was going to the Great City! He moved in a daze of excitement, scarcely able to think of anything but the adventure which lay before him. It surprised and amused him that Zolic was in favor of their going to the big market to sell their wares, for he had so long been set against the thing called money. But even Zolic had to admit that people could not eat fine lacquer or serapes, and in this region there was no food to exchange for such things. Under these circumstances, he said, it was necessary to go forth to the place where food could be found.

Once Zolic had made this decision, the Olina family worked almost night and day to make more and finer things to take to the Great City. Even Tara and

Marina were put to work polishing the lacquer pieces.
Now and then Tara tried his hand at etching designs
on the less perfect gourds, for soon it would be time
that he learned this skill which had been carried on
in the family for generations.

The *lacas* made by the Olinas had won wide fame
and Zolic would not allow their making to be cheapened by using paints that could be bought in a store,
as some of his neighbors did. The Olinas still used
earth and plant colors as their ancestors had in the
olden days, so their *lacas* had the distinctive and pecul-
iar yellows, pinks, greens, and blues which could not
be bought, but had to be carefully sought out and
mixed with plant oils. The brilliant red color came
from the red cochineal bug that lives on the cactus
plants; the lacquer itself was mixed with oil from a
worm called gie.

First, the surface of the piece was painted over with
black lacquer, and then allowed to dry. Afterwards
it was polished with the palm of the hand until it had
a fine sheen. At this stage, the design was traced with
a sharp instrument by Zolic or Chalma. Then the
women rubbed colors into the pattern with brushes or
their thumbs. The final polishing could be done by
Tara and Marina, if they were careful.

All of the pieces were called *lacas,* but each shape
has its special name. A half gourd which makes a bowl
is a *jícara*. The large, flat part of an enormous gourd

used as a platter is a *batea*. The gourd with a little
lid to it is called a *tecomate*.

Sometimes Tara and Marina grew tired of polishing and were allowed to use extra gourds for their
own designs. They delighted in fashioning little birds,
using fat round shapes for the bodies and little pointed
ones for heads, sometimes finding ones with thin
curved stems for necks. They glued these together,
after having lacquered them. Each bird was given
thin legs made of sticks and a sharp thorn for a bill.

One day Tara found a gourd that was well shaped
but too small for making anything for market. He
managed to cut it so that it had a neatly fitting lid, as
did the family heirloom, the *tecomate* with the golden
bird. He decided to experiment with this piece. He
carefully lacquered it with black, then got out the
golden-bird bowl and tried to copy its design. Zolic
came along and saw what he was doing. He snatched
the golden bird *tecomate* away from him.

"What are you doing?" he roared.

"Trying to copy the golden bird," Tara said, looking up in surprise at the anger on his grandfather's
face.

"Why do you think that I myself have never tried
to copy this loveliest of designs?" the old man asked.

"Why?"

"Because it is sacred. To make many of them would
cheapen this piece. Lessen its powers as a good luck

charm. There is only one such *tecomate*. Keep it precious."

Zolic took the gourd upon which Tara had been working, dashed it to the ground, and crushed it with a rock. Then he, himself, put the precious golden bird away.

The days dragged by. Tara could scarcely wait until the time when they should set out on the great adventure — the journey to the Great City. Each day he anxiously scanned the sky for clouds, fearing that if they did not start soon, the rains would come and the crops would grow and the need for the trip would be gone.

The Great Adventure

At LAST the great day came — the day about which Tara had been dreaming for so long.

They were all up before dawn. Everyone, even the grandparents, helped to load onto the two burros the packed lacquer ware, the fine *rebozos* and serapes, the tiny amount of ground corn and beans, and the small brazier which would serve as their stove. A small supply of food was left behind. Everyone would go hungry before more food was earned in the Great City.

The big day was not the way Tara had first dreamed it would be. He had imagined himself alone astride Diablo setting out to see the outside world. But this way was better. Having his father and mother along for company would be pleasant. He was actually going on the trip to the Great City and that was the main thing. If it hadn't been for Diablo, perhaps he would not have been taken at all. Since Chalma and Cheran were using his burro to carry a load, it was only right that he, Diablo's owner, should go along.

While they ate a hurried and meager breakfast Tara

chattered of the adventure this would be — of the
sights he would see. Then, for no good reason at all
the thought which had long been deep in his mind
bubbled up in words.

"Maybe I'll find what I am looking for."

"Are you looking for something, my son?" Chalma
asked, his manner indifferent. It seemed that he
scarcely heard, but Zolic was quick to sense what was
in Tara's mind.

"Yes, you are looking for something," he said, and
there was the force behind his words which had made
him for so long the spiritual leader of this Tarascan
settlement. "Everyone should be a searcher — looking
for something which will tell him the meaning of his
own life. Most people forever search for something
they have lost or maybe never found. Yet the something each man searches for lies deep within himself."

Tara frowned. He did not know just what the Wise
One meant, but he was sure that what he was looking
for must be far away. Otherwise he might as well
stay at home — and that he did not want to do.

Zolic's piercing eyes were on him, making him
squirm. Finally the Wise One said, "No matter. You
will know when you find it. You are one set apart.
Your destiny will be made plain in good time."

Tara nodded, indulging the old man. Zolic often
spoke in riddles. It was a way he had.

The burros were packed. They were nearly ready
to go. Cheran went to the cabinet and took out the

fine *tecomate* with the golden bird traced upon it. "Take this." She held it out to Tara. "Wear it under your shirt. It carries good fortune with it, you know."

Tara filled it with water and was putting the lid on when Kalli the Good One came shuffling in. Over her arm was a folded serape. It was of a lovely deep blue and across the middle was the same design as was on the precious bowl — a golden bird.

Tara caught in his breath. Never had he seen so fine a serape as this.

"It will bring many pesos on the market place," he cried.

He saw from the look in the eyes of Zolic and Kalli that he had said the wrong thing.

Zolic remarked, "Many things are beyond money. Beauty is something to treasure. We may be hungry, but we will never sell the golden bird *tecomate* you carry under your shirt, nor must you ever part with this serape. It is the finest work Kalli has ever done — the climax of the work of her lifetime. She will not be here much longer. But this piece of weaving will keep you warm all of your days, and it will delight your eyes and soul. After you are gone, it will pass on to your oldest son, and then to his."

Tara could understand these words of the Wise One. They did not make a riddle. Beauty was beyond price. It would be better to go hungry than to part with these precious things into which so much loving labor had gone.

"I will keep this serape forever," he said. "It and the golden bird *tecomate* will always be my treasures."

Zolic nodded approvingly. "The golden bird is the symbol of the blood of kings. The golden bird will someday lead you to your heart's desire."

Tara smiled politely. Now Zolic was talking in riddles again.

"Come," Chalma called. "We must get started."

Zolic, Kalli, and Marina stood watching them set off down the trail. Marina, of course, cradled the new baby in her dark *rebozo*. Tara saw the mist in her

eyes and felt sorry that she must remain behind. He was glad that he was not a girl.

"Tie the dog until we are out of sight," Chalma told Marina. "He would only make trouble."

It was a long journey, but Tara was seldom tired

because his interest in all they passed kept his mind from any bodily discomforts. They traveled along a great highway on a dusty path beside the smooth black road over which the fine cars of the tourists whizzed in a steady stream.

Now and then one of the automobiles stopped and it was instantly surrounded by a throng of ragged Mexican boys and girls who seemed to come from nowhere. All held hands outstretched for cincos. But Tara did not join these begging crowds, for Cheran and Chalma would not have allowed it even if he had wanted to.

They passed other small caravans of laden burros and their drivers on the way to some market, or returning from one. There were young men on bicycles wherever they went, and Tara marveled that they were not hit by the speeding automobiles. Men, women, and girls trudged along barefoot, with water jars or great baskets balanced on their heads. Often Tara saw men, too poor to own burros, who had loaded themselves with heavy burdens.

There were lofty mountains, deep valleys, and farms clinging to the hillsides. Every day brought new and wonderful things to see. Tara felt that now he was really living. It was as well that they were afoot, for, although the going was slow and wearying, this mode of travel gave them plenty of time to enjoy the sights. Tara wondered how the people rushing by in automobiles were able to see anything at all.

The weather grew cooler as they climbed higher; the skies were blue again, not faded as they had been at home. Beauty lay on every side. Great mountains pushed against the clouds and all about was every sort of tree, fruit, shrub, or flower in the world, Tara was sure.

At last they were inside the Great City. A man in a blue uniform stopped them at the big gate and tried to tell them the route they must go. Chalma could not understand the man's language, but Tara had picked up enough Spanish so that he could piece together what the man was saying.

"I know the way we must go to get our burros to the market place," Chalma said when Tara had finished his job of interpreting. "I was here when you were but a babe."

They had to skirt the city. This disappointed Tara, but his father told him that toward the middle of town there were so many cars that it would have been impossible to drive the burros through the crowded streets.

Nor were they allowed to drive the burros all the way to the market place. They were stopped at another entrance where they were told that they could come in, but that they would have to leave their burros outside. The stiff-looking official told them that they could leave the animals at a stable nearby — or turn them out to graze — the boy could stay to herd them.

At this Tara was tempted to raise a loud wail. Instead he said, "But how will we get our goods to the market, *señor?* If you would allow us to let our burros carry the things in, I could lead them outside again after they are unloaded."

"It is not allowed," the man said. "Do as the others do. Load the goods on your backs. Turn the burros loose. They will graze along the roadside."

"But someone might steal them," Tara protested.

The official spread his hands and shrugged. "Most likely not. But if they are stolen, what matter? You take someone else's. A burro is a burro."

"Mine," Tara said, "is a very special burro. I would not trade him for all the other burros in Mexico."

"I cannot stand here arguing," the officer said crossly. "Be on your way."

Chalma, Cheran, and Tara stared at each other helplessly. What to do now? Suddenly Tara wished he were back among the little circle of adobe houses with the climbing camelina, which was home — or on the lake with Lucio. Life in the Great City was too terrifying and difficult for poor and simple people.

They moved on a short distance to get out of range of the angry glare the officer had turned on them. "It may be best to do as he says," Chalma finally spoke. "Leave the burros outside the city to graze and carry the goods into market on our backs."

"I will not leave Diablo," Tara cried out.

"We are leaving Toto," his father said. "It is the best we can do. As the officer said, there are other burros. We saw many grazing beside the road. If someone takes ours, we will just consider it an exchange — and take theirs."

Tara pulled on the bridle rein to stop Diablo and he planted himself by the road with his legs far apart. "I will not part with Diablo. Toto's just like any of the others we saw. But my burro is different. I will not lose him. I will stay here on the edge of the city and care for the animals, then. You two go into the market." He wondered if Diablo realized what a tremendous sacrifice he was making.

"But Cheran and I can't carry the burdens of two burros on our own backs," Chalma pointed out. "And we must get our goods to the market to keep ourselves and our people from starving. Is your burro more important than our welfare?"

Tara swallowed hard. Of course he could not stand out against such an argument. He started loosening the packs on Diablo's back. As he did so he whispered into the black burro's ear. "Don't let anyone else take you or ride you. You are mine. I'll be back for you in two or three days — as soon as we get our goods sold. If anyone tries to ride you — *sit down*."

Diablo twitched one ear knowingly.

Soon the three travelers had taken all the packs off the burros and laid them out on the ground. As though they understood what was expected of them, the burros moved a short distance from the road and started cropping the grass. Diablo did not even look at Tara.

The packs were divided into three parts, the smaller one being fastened on to Cheran's back. It made Tara's heart ache to see her set off along the road bent under her burden. He helped load a heavier pack on his father's back, then Chalma lifted the last pack and fastened it around Tara's shoulders with rope.

Tara grinned at his father as he set off at a fast pace. "Now I know how it feels to be a burro," he said. "He-haw. He-haw."

"Save your strength, my son," Chalma advised.

Lost!

TARA AND HIS FAMILY reached the market place and made arrangements for a space as most of the people were going home. The Olinas would have to roll up in their serapes and spend the night right there. They had nowhere else to go. Soon Cheran had the handful of charcoal burning under the brazier and the smell of cooking *tortillas* and beans filled the air. By the time the last cart had clattered away, they were asleep beside their packs of goods, which they would not spread out before daylight.

The next morning they arose early and arranged the handsome lacquer ware and fine serapes for display. For breakfast they each had one *tortilla* — it was the last of their food. Tara ate his slowly, to make it last. Suddenly he had an idea. "I think I could sell many of the *rebozos* if I took them over my arm and walked about the streets," he said.

"It sounds like a wise idea," Cheran agreed.

Chalma gave the boy a piercing look. "You wouldn't be saying this because you would like to get out and see the sights?"

"We-ell, partly," Tara admitted with a grin. "But I do really think I could sell them that way."

"It is a good idea," Chalma said. "All three of us will not be needed to manage the stall here. I will wait and see how things go, then perhaps I will take some of the serapes out on the street and try to sell them to the tourists. Cheran can stay here and tend to the selling of the lacquer ware. Perhaps that way we can sell our goods faster and set out for home tomorrow."

At these words Tara stiffened. He had not wanted his plan to turn out this way. He wanted time — much time to see the Great City. He could not possibly do it all in one short day. Yet, what about Diablo? It was important that no one stole this finest of burros. He picked up the neatly folded *rebozos* and put them over one arm.

"Take the golden bird *tecomate* and your new serape," his mother reminded him. "The golden bird will bring you good fortune in selling the Good One's *rebozos*. The serape will keep you and the *rebozos* dry if a sudden rain should come up."

Tara smiled at her as he picked up the precious bowl and walked over to fill it at the place where a pipe rose from the ground. All he had to do to get water was to turn a handle. It was the most wonderful contrivance he had ever seen. He put the lid back on the bowl and hung it by its cord over his shoulder and under his other arm beneath his shirt. He laid the folded new serape over one shoulder in the way all Mexican countrymen wore theirs.

Tara set out, walking quickly, but his steps soon slowed, for right here at hand in the big market were such wonders as he had never imagined. There were stacks of shoes and sandals; piles of sombreros, beautiful serapes and *rebozos* — although none were so fine as those made by his mother and grandmother. And the food! The delicious odors made his mouth water, for all along the street women were bent over their *braseros* cooking. Pyramids of bright oranges, piles of bananas and coconuts, bowls of golden honey, plumes of pepper berries, small cords of sugar cane — every kind of fruit Tara had ever tasted and many he had never seen before lined the market place. He turned away. Hunger gnawed at his stomach.

He came to the flower market and paused. Never had he hoped to see such a thing. Surely every sort of flower was sold here — tall ones standing erect and proud in high containers, with shorter-stemmed varieties in front, and all along the entire line flower arrangements that were incredibly lovely.

There were many displays of pottery, but nowhere did Tara see anything to compare with the quality of the Olina *lacas*.

He left the market and found himself surrounded by towering buildings. As yet the streets were quiet. People were beginning to straggle into the market place with their wares to sell, but no one was buying.

Only a few cars moved on the street. Tara peered into the windows, marveling at such magnificence and wealth. The beauty and size of the buildings amazed him. He came to a great square on the opposite side of which stood a massive cathedral. It was beautiful. How could men have built such a place? It must surely be the most wonderful building in the whole world.

Tara was so inspired with awe that he stood staring at the cathedral until people began to bump into him as the street became busier and more crowded.

Now cars were passing in all directions and it really became dangerous to cross the streets. Tara's method was to run as fast as he could, darting between the cars. Horns shrieked and drivers leaned out of their windows to yell at him. Tara knew no other method of crossing a street, although now and then he was surprised when suddenly all cars stopped and people on foot streamed across the intersections.

Once, in one of his dashes, he came so near to being hit that the fender of the car actually brushed him. Instinctively he turned away just in time, but the back of his shirt was torn. This near-accident made him more careful and reminded him of the man from his village who had been hit by an automobile and had not walked since. Now he proceeded more slowly, waiting with the crowd at the corners and walking across when they did, although he could not figure out how they knew when to stop and when to go.

Finally he had walked so far that his feet hurt and he was hungry. Only then did he remember that he had set out to sell the *rebozos* which had now become so heavy on his arm.

He was on a long parkway which divided a wide street into two parts. There were benches to sit on, and Tara sank down upon one of them and held his aching feet out straight in front of him. He didn't know if he had a right to sit here, but no one seemed inclined to run him off.

He slid the *rebozos* from his arm. Then he drew the *tecomate* from beneath his shirt and drank from it. The water was warmish, but it wetted his parched mouth and throat.

As he was drinking, a car which had been going by slowly stopped just in front of him and a lady, plainly an American, leaned from the window and, pointing to his *tecomate,* talked rapidly and in an excited manner. Tara could not grasp anything she said, for she was an *americano.*

The man who was driving and another lady, evidently his *señora,* stepped from the car, as did the American lady. The other two people looked like wealthy Mexicans. The man spoke to Tara in Spanish, but so fast that Tara could not understand.

Tara shrugged. He wished the people would go away. He hastily put the lid back on the *tecomate* and thrust it under his shirt. At this the American lady began to jabber fast and loud. The man pointed a finger at the bulge in Tara's shirt and spoke more slowly. Tara understood that the lady wanted to buy his *tecomate*. That she would pay many pesos for it.

Tara shook his head. Then he picked up the *rebozos* and stood up. He thrust them forward and tried to say that they were for sale. Very lovely *rebozos*.

Both of the women picked up *rebozo* ends and carefully examined the work. It was evident that they were well pleased, for they talked excitedly and pointed out the fine work. It seemed that they were especially impressed by the lovely designs woven into the ends above the fringe.

"How much?" the man demanded.

Tara told them the price his father had set.

"Too much," the man said in Spanish. Tara understood him and thought the matter settled. He started to fold the *rebozos* neatly.

But the women's chatter commenced again. The man named a lower price. Tara shook his head. The man named another price. Tara repeated the price he had asked at first.

"Here's a little beggar I can't bargain with," the man said in Spanish to his *señora*. Tara caught the meaning and his face grew hot.

"I am not a beggar," he said in his halting Spanish. "My grandmother worked hard to make these *rebozos*. We sell them at a fair price."

More rapid conversation passed among the three, and finally the man drew out a fat wallet and began to count bills. Tara's eyes grew large. It was amazing that one person could possess so much money. This man must be very rich. Tara held out his hand and the man put a heap of bills in it with several coins on top. Surely one *rebozo* could not bring this much money! Then the man lifted all of the garments from his arm. He was buying the whole lot.

The *señora* said to her husband, "How wonderful! Now she has presents for all her American friends."

Tara stood for some time watching the car go down the street. So this was one of the rich *touristas* Lucio and Pepe had told him about. She was so rich that she bought his whole store of *rebozos*. How pleased his parents would be. But if they had been as lucky in selling their lacquer ware, this visit to the Great City would be over all too soon. It had scarcely begun.

Tara darted across the street to the side on which were many fine shops and he stared into them in wonderment. Some of the stores showed nothing but gleaming silver of all sizes and shapes which he guessed must be used by the rich. Some sold ladies' dresses, and others fabrics or furniture; still others were filled with many small items for which Tara could not even guess the uses.

Finally he came to a tiny shop. In it sat several women engaged in an occupation that gave Tara a severe twinge of homesickness. They were picking up little balls of cornmeal dough and slapping them back and forth, back and forth, to make thin round sheets.

Then they cooked the tiny sheets — or *tortillas* — on a stove, and the delicious aroma made Tara feel slightly faint.

He walked up the street a short distance debating with himself. He had a pocket bulging with money. But was he entitled to spend any of it for food for himself?

He walked entirely around the block without deciding the matter. Then he came back to the little shop where the rhythmic slap, slapping sound still went on and the warm odor of cooking *tortillas* wafted to his nostrils. He made up his mind that it would be all right for him to spend some of the small coins.

He dug out two pieces of money and put them on the counter, pointing to the pile of warm *tortillas* which had just come from the stove. One of the young women smiled at him and put several of them in a paper sack, which she handed to him.

Tara darted back across the street to the parkway and sat on the grass, wriggling his toes in its coolness as he munched the delicious *tortillas*. He ate them, every one, then took out his *tecomate* to drink again. He emptied the water and decided that this bowl, hidden under his shirt, would be a fine place to store the wealth he had acquired so suddenly and unexpectedly.

"The Wise One said the golden bird would bring me luck," he reminded himself. "It has already — helping me to sell the *rebozos* so fast."

He stuffed the bills inside the golden-bird bowl and replaced the lid before he thrust it under his shirt again. Rested, and his strength renewed by the life-giving corn of the *tortillas,* he got up, stretched, and went about his sightseeing. Since he had sold his wares so quickly, he was sure that his parents would not mind his doing as he pleased for the rest of the day. Surely they would not be so fortunate as to sell all of the *lacas* and the serapes in one morning. He hoped not. Perhaps tomorrow he could take some of the serapes and sell them to tourists. But before he went to sleep tonight he would walk to the edge of the city and see how Diablo was getting along. For some reason he no longer worried about him. Diablo was smart enough to take care of himself.

Tara wandered about the streets staring and having the most marvelous time he had ever known. But now the air was cooling. A stiff breeze came up. The sun was out of sight and the light was growing dim. Tara finally decided that he had better make his way back to the market place. He hurried his steps. Then it dawned on him that it could not be this way. There was nothing here he had seen before.

He stopped at a street corner to try to get his bearings. But he was in an utterly strange world. Panic seized him. He realized that he was lost!

Where Am I?

THE MARKET PLACE? Where is the market place?"
Frantically he asked the question of everyone he met.
The strangers only stared at him with blank eyes. He
was using his own tongue — Tarascan words. In his
panic, he did not remember the Spanish words for
the place he was seeking, although he had once known
them. He had been so proud of the Spanish expres-
sions he had picked up from Pepe and Lucio — but
now they were not enough to make known his terrible
need.

Finally he remembered the word he had heard used
when he helped drive the banana train to the city.
"*Zocolo? Zocolo?*" he cried to each stranger who ap-
proached. Some of them hurried by as if afraid or
suspicious of him.

Finally one man stopped and glowered at him
darkly, then pointed in the opposite direction from
which Tara had been traveling. Tara turned and
started to run in that direction. Now there were few
people walking, although cars with bright lights still
sped up and down the wide avenue. Metal blinds had

been drawn over most of the shop windows. The streets were dark and gloomy.

He ran until he was out of breath, then he stopped and finally sank onto a dark doorstep. Where was he? Surely this could not be the way to the *zocolo,* or big square. If he could only find the central part of the city, he felt that he might be able to pick his way to the market.

Suddenly such a longing to see his parents swept over him that it made him ill. Oh, why had he been so headstrong — so bent upon seeing all of this new world that he failed to take his bearings?

In the hills and valleys around his home place he had learned always to take notice of landmarks and sight his direction with the sun. Yet here in this strange new world he had plunged ahead and gone around countless blocks until now he was hopelessly confused and lost.

He was in a district of fine houses, where lights shone warmly from windows. Yet all of these houses were surrounded by strong iron fences or high solid walls. He knew that he had not passed such a district before. Surely he must be going in the wrong direction. He turned and retraced his steps, hurrying back to the point where he had been when the man directed him. Then he stopped and looked all around him. He started walking again but shortly found himself in another section where older houses lined the streets, all forbiddingly shut off by walls and iron bars.

A cold wind had come up. Tara shivered. Suddenly he remembered the serape his mother had insisted that he take — the beautiful blue serape with the golden bird design. Gratefully he unfolded it and thrust his head through the slit in the middle, and felt for a moment that the wings of the golden bird were sheltering and protecting him.

Before long, though, all strength seemed to drain from his legs. He was wearier than he had ever been in his life before. In spite of the serape over his shoulders he trembled with cold — or was it with fear? Every bone ached with tiredness and he was hungry, thirsty and completely miserable.

Stumbling along he noticed a step before one of the gateways and he saw that the gate itself was hidden within a little recess. To Tara it made a shelter of sorts and he sank down upon the steps and huddled against the wall. How foolish he had been to eat all of the *tortillas* at once. And why had he not been wise enough to refill his *tecomate* with water at the fountain when he had been in the parkway? Now his bowl was stuffed with bills from the sale of his *rebozos*.

At the time this unexpected sale had been like a miracle. But what good was a bowl full of money? He could not eat or drink the bills, nor were they any help in keeping him warm.

Tara was being shaken until his head wobbled. Dazed with sleep he stared up at a man who was glowering at him angrily. A rapid flow of Spanish words came from the man's lips. Tara understood that he was being told to go away.

He got to his feet and started running. When his breath was coming in gasps he looked over his shoulder, but the street was empty. No one was chasing him.

Attracted by a bright, warm-looking light to his left, he turned to cross the street. There was a sudden roaring sound, screeching of brakes, horn blaring, and a blinding light; then complete and blank darkness.

Tara opened his eyes and stared about at clean white walls. He was lying on something smooth and soft. His hands plucked at the white cloth which covered him. He found himself on the first real bed upon which he had ever lain. Along the walls was a row of similar beds. Some of them were empty but others held boys of various ages.

Tara sat up and blinked his eyes. "Where am I?" he demanded.

The heads all turned in his direction and eyes stared at him curiously. "My mother and father, where are they?" he asked.

Still the eyes stared and no answer came from any of the mouths. Then Tara realized that he had been speaking in his own tongue.

"Where am I?" he tried slowly in Spanish.

The boy on the cot next to him spoke up, "We are the forgotten ones," he said. His tone was hopeless and he turned his head away. The others, too, turned away or went back to staring at the ceiling or the wall.

Those words and the hopeless tone in which they were spoken sent a chill through Tara. The forgotten ones? What did that mean? Had he died and gone to the City of the Dead? What had happened?

Weak and dizzy he sank back on the pillow. He held up his hand and stared at it. It looked thin and very clean. But he could wiggle his fingers. Surely, then, he must be alive.

Finally, over a period of days, remembrance came back slowly, piece by piece, but hazily, as though in a dream — the blinding lights, the noise, the pit of darkness from which he tried time after time to clamber into the light. But with each glimpse of light came such hideous pain in his head that he was glad to ease back into the blackness where pain was blotted out. Yet that blackness was filled with nightmares.

Time after time he dreamed of being chased by a car with harsh stabbing lights as he raced toward his father and his mother who stood with outstretched arms. Then always came the crash.

He groaned at the terrible memories and rolled his head from side to side. Once more he opened his eyes. He was still in the long white room with the rows of beds. The pain in his head was less intense. He did not sink back into the pit of blackness where nightmares lurked.

He kept his eyes open, wondering what had happened and where he was. He now realized that he had been hit by a car, but how did he come to be in this place? Where were his parents? And where was Diablo?

At the thought of them it was as though a giant hand had seized his heart and was squeezing it. He was one big pang of longing for his parents, yet his greatest worry was for Diablo. Chalma and Cheran could take care of themselves. But it was certain that someone would steal Diablo. Anyone could see by looking at him what a remarkable burro he was.

A lady came into the room dressed in white from the tip of her cap to her shoes. She passed along the row of beds, speaking to each occupant, stroking the foreheads of some, putting a tiny, slim glass stick into the mouths of others, and holding some by the wrist.

When she came to Tara's cot he stared up at her, feeling half defiant, half fearful.

"Well, hello!" she said. "So you're awake?"

"Where am I?" he demanded.

"Well," she said in a cheerful tone. "You are ready to see the doctor."

She walked away briskly, but in a few moments returned pushing what looked like a chair on wheels. She put her arms under Tara's shoulders and helped him to rise. Then carefully she lifted him into the chair which she rolled through the long room and into another room where a man sat behind a wide table. He smiled and instantly Tara's fear melted. Here, he thought, was a friend. Goodness and kindness came from this man as warmth from the sun. His gray eyes were wide-set and Tara felt they had the power to probe his deepest thoughts — yet they were the most understanding eyes Tara had ever seen. They reminded him of the eyes of the Good One.

"I am glad to see you." The man's voice was deep but kind. He spoke slowly.

"Where am I?" Tara asked.

"You are in the Boys' Club. Can you understand my words?"

Tara nodded.

"Do you speak Spanish?"

Tara held the tips of his thumb and forefinger nearly touching, indicating that he spoke only a little of the language.

"But you understand this much." The man smiled and held his hands apart.

Tara nodded and smiled back hesitantly.

"I am Doctor Brito," the man spoke slowly and clearly. "Every night I go out on the streets and pick up the forgotten ones and bring them here to teach and help."

"I am not forgotten!" Tara struggled for words. "I got lost from my father and mother," he managed in a mixture of Spanish and Tarascan.

The doctor nodded understandingly. He seemed to grasp Tara's thought. "It happens so often. I have picked up hundreds like you, but many can speak no Spanish at all, nor understand it. What is your name?"

"Tara. Tara Olina."

"Where are you from?"

Tara shook his head.

The doctor tried again. "Where is your home?"

"By the lake."

"What is the name of the lake?"

Again Tara shook his head. Perhaps it had a name but he and the others had always called it the lake.

"My father and mother will take me there," he said. "They know the way. I must get to the market place. They are waiting for me. They will be worried."

In his excitement he slid to the edge of the chair. Then at sight of the puzzled frown on the doctor's face Tara realized that he had been speaking in his native tongue.

He strained for Spanish words to convey his meaning. He tried so hard that it made his head hurt. Oh, why hadn't he made Pepe and Lucio talk to him more in Spanish?

The doctor's eyes grew soft with pity. "It's no use," he said slowly. "We must wait until you know more of our language. Try hard to understand what I say. You have been here this many days." He held up both hands with fingers outstretched to indicate ten days.

That long! Tara gasped. Would his parents wait that long at the market place?

"A car hit you," the doctor went on. "You got a bad gash on your head." He pointed to Tara's wound. "You were unconscious — asleep for ten days."

He handed Tara a shiny square which gave him back his image as the lake did when it was smooth. Tara saw that his hair had been cut off and was now short and bristly. Slanting across his forehead was a red mark, showing a deep scar which had healed over. Yes, it would have taken many days for such a deep cut to heal as much as this had done.

"But my father and mother must still be waiting at the market place," he insisted. "I must hurry there." He half rose, then sank back, partly because of weakness, partly because of the feeling of hopelessness which swept over him. He realized that his parents could not wait this long. They would have returned to Zolic and the Good One, to Marina and the baby. The kind doctor was the only one in the world who could help him and between them stood the terrible barrier created because they could not speak the same language. He was, however, able to understand much more than he was able to put forth.

His hand clutched the edge of the chair. "My *tecomate* with the golden bird?" he cried. "Where is it? Who has taken it? It was full of money. And the blue serape? It was the finest Kalli ever made."

"I don't understand." The doctor smiled. His eyes studied Tara's face.

"My *tecomate!*" Tara's hands formed the round outline of the bowl. "The golden bird." His hands fluttered like a bird's wings.

The doctor's features lighted up with understanding. He rose and went to a cabinet, which he unlocked. He drew forth the bowl with the golden bird and the blue serape.

"Are these what you are talking about?"

Tara grabbed his belongings.

The doctor let him hold them for a time, then he gently took them away.

"So much money?" he said when he lifted the lid of the bowl. He gave Tara a questioning look.

Tara spoke rapidly, trying to tell him about the American woman who had bought all of his *rebozos,* but of course the man could not understand. He put the things back into the cabinet and locked the door.

"Learn to speak Spanish, Tara," he said gently. "Then I am sure we will be able to find your people."

"*Zocolo! Zocolo!*" Tara could remember the Spanish words. "My people are waiting for me."

It seemed to him that if he said this often enough and loud enough it would make it true.

The doctor pushed a button on his desk and like magic the lady in the white dress came in. The doctor spoke to her. She left the room and soon returned carrying blue trousers and shirt, which she handed to Tara with motions for him to put them on. He did so. Meantime the doctor pushed another button. Tara was quickly wheeled in the chair through two doors which swung open when they were pushed, and out into the cool clear night air. A long car, which made Tara think of the buses he had seen along the highway, was standing beside the door. The doctor took his arm and helped him climb into the seat next to the driver. The doctor sat on Tara's other side.

When the long car began to move it seemed to Tara that they were traveling faster than the wind and as smoothly as if they were riding on a cloud. How amazed his father and mother would be to see him riding up in such style!

There were not many people walking on the streets, but there were many cars. Now they were passing the great cathedral that had astonished Tara so on his first morning in the Great City. His heart beat quickened at the sight of things he had seen before. Soon they were at the market place, but it was quiet, as it had been the first night Tara spent there.

"My mother and father are asleep," he said. "They stay by their *lacas,* so no one will steal them."

He looked toward the place where they had set up their stand when they arrived, but now that place was occupied by heaps of cheap pottery and beside them snored a fat old man.

"They must have moved. . . . " Tara's voice trailed off.

Slowly the car drove along the street lined by the empty stalls of the market place.

"They sold their *lacas,*" Tara said finally. "Just as I sold the *rebozos.* Right away. The goods my people make are very fine. People would buy them as soon as they saw them."

"Tara," the doctor said. "You must try to understand. Your father and mother are not here. They have gone home. They would be frightened — bewildered. Maybe they waited a few days. Then they must have gone home."

Tara covered his face with his hands. He had no words for this terrible thing that had happened to him. Not only was he deserted by his parents, but now surely Diablo was lost to him forever.

He felt the doctor's arm slide about him and his head was drawn to the firm shoulder.

The kind voice said softly, "This seems like an awful blow to you now, Tara. Yet it may turn out to be the best thing that ever happened to you — as it has to so many of our lost ones. Try to be brave. Things will work out for you, believe me."

Strange New World

Weeks and months went by in this strange new world in which Tara found himself. Every day for one full round of the moon he went into the schoolroom, where he was first drilled in speaking the Spanish language. Then he learned to read Spanish words printed in white chalk on a black board. Then he read black words printed on white cards. Finally he was handed a book with the black letters in long lines. These lines made sentences. And the sentences added together made a story.

Suddenly a wonderful thrill ran through Tara. He could read! From a book. The walls of the schoolroom were lined with books in lovely bright colors. Those books were like other new worlds. He determined to read every one. Learning was fun. He soaked up knowledge as the thirsty desert soaked up the rain.

The terrible, longing ache for his own people never completely left him, but in time it did ease enough so that he was not actually sick as he had been at first. Strangely enough, he still missed Diablo more than he did his people. Diablo had belonged especially to him. Between them had been a particular bond. Tara knew he would never find another burro to equal him.

Many of the boys — the waifs that the good doctor picked up in his wanderings over the streets of the city — at first knew no Spanish at all. Many of them were, like Tara, from some remote Indian village, and knew only their native tongue. Some, like Tara, had been accidentally lost; others had been deliberately and cruelly abandoned.

When Tara had mastered the language well enough to get along among strange people he became a shoeshine boy and was taught how to go out into the city and say brightly to men passing by, "Shoeshine, *señor?*"

He had a little kit containing shoeshine materials slung over his shoulder and he proudly wore a badge saying he was a member of the Boys' Club. Thus he learned the fine satisfaction which comes from being self-supporting. He bought his own clothes from the store connected with the club and paid for his own meals. It surprised him to find how proud he felt to be earning his own way.

As soon as he was given the freedom of the streets he thought about finding the road by which he entered the city. When he found it he would return to his people. Every day he ventured farther from the Boys' Club, getting lost several times. But now that he could speak Spanish there was always someone to be found who would show him the way. Every day he took a different direction, hoping to locate the way he had come in.

Luis, one of his fellow shoeshine boys, told him that it was useless to try to find his parents. "There are hundreds of roads coming into the Great City from all directions," he said. "And into each of them come many other roads. You could never find it. Besides — why bother? Your parents don't want you. They probably lost you on purpose, like mine did." His jaw set in a firm line and his eyes grew hard.

Tara stared at Luis for a long moment. It was on the tip of his tongue to cry out that he had not been abandoned or forgotten. He was sure of it. But he bit back the words. They would be cruel in the face of Luis' certainty that he had been deserted. Tara knew of other boys like him.

In time he began to realize the hopelessness of finding the road leading to his home. He asked the taxicab drivers, who know the city better than anyone else, but none of them could help him. They told him that the Great City was like the center of a spider web with roads going from it every which way. It would be foolish for him to try to set out on foot. He would be an old man before he reached his goal.

Finally he realized that he must wait. So he went on, working to earn his living each day and every evening studying two hours in the schoolroom of the Boys' Club.

One day Tio, as the boys called their beloved doctor, called him into the library — a cozy room with a cheery fire in the fireplace and with the colorful, book-lined walls. Tara perched on the edge of the chair the doctor motioned to him and stared around at the wealth of books and the fine pictures.

"You are doing well, Tara," the doctor said, leaning on the desk and smiling in a friendly fashion. "In fact, you are surprising your teacher in the speed with which you have learned to read. Books are wonderful friends, you know. They are like windows, opening new worlds. I am glad that you have taken so well to reading."

"I never saw a book until I came here." Tara forgot his shyness in the doctor's friendly manner. "I want to read every book in the world."

"That's a lot of books." The doctor's kind eyes studied him. "Your teacher tells me you have a good mind. Perhaps you will turn out to be one of our special ones."

"Special ones?" Tara did not grasp the doctor's meaning.

Tio nodded. "We have cared for hundreds of *los olvidados* — the forgotten ones. Most of them learn to read and write and to become self-supporting. But that is as far as many of them advance. It is something — it keeps them from being beggars or thieves. Once in a while a special one turns up — one who has in him the seeds of leadership. One who can go back to his people and show them the way to a better life. They become teachers, perhaps. Your teacher is one of the special ones — a waif whom I picked up on the streets, cold and half starved. I have others like him in many parts of the country. You may remember that once I said perhaps your accident would be the

best thing that ever happened to you — it has opened
the doors to a new world."

For a moment it was as though Tio's words had
kindled a spark in Tara's heart. Warmth and excitement ran through him. Then suddenly the feeling
vanished, for there came to him the picture of Zolic
bent over his lacquer work.

"My grandfather — they call him the Wise One —
always said that the old ways were best. That only evil
comes from our people trying to take on the new ways
— that when men become greedy after money all that
is good in their hearts dies. Many people have become beggars and thieves in order to get money."

The doctor smiled understandingly. "Money does
bring out the bad in some men. But it's not money
itself which is evil; it's what men do to get it, or the
use they make of it. In itself it's merely a handy
medium of exchange. More simple than bartering
with goods. And it may be a tool for either good or
evil, depending on how men use it. I could not run
this Boys' Club without money. Many people help
by giving money and in this use money is a force for
good."

Tara widened his eyes. This was a new and deep
thought which he must ponder, to understand its
meaning.

"Yet," Dr. Brito went on, "there is truth in what
your Wise One says about the old ways being good.
You are an Indian, Tara. Never be ashamed of that.

Although since the coming of the white man the Indians of Mexico have been treated like people of low caste, actually they are descendants of noble races among whom were great artists, architects, and astronomers. They were the builders of strange and wonderful civilizations. It is this nobility and the fine artistry of these races which are in danger of being lost."

Tara blinked. He was able to grasp the good doctor's meaning, yet the idea was so big and deep that it would take much thinking to digest it.

"Many of these native races had unusually fine arts and crafts," the doctor went on. "Some of these are being cheapened by the urge to turn things out in too great a hurry to satisfy the tourist demand."

"That is what the Wise One meant." Tara straightened up. "For as long back as anyone can remember his family has made the most beautiful *lacas* in the world. And my mother and grandmother weave fine *rebozos* and serapes. But it is the lacquer ware that is very special."

He went on to describe the method of its making, now and then lapsing into his own native tongue in his haste to tell about it. Then he straightened up and said eagerly, "Where is my *tecomate* — the black bowl with the golden bird? And my serape? If you see these again you will believe me."

The doctor drew out a bunch of keys and went to a cabinet, which he unlocked. On one of the shelves Tara's gourd rested on the folded serape. The things were labeled with his name and number. The doctor took them down and placed them on his desk. Then he picked up the *tecomate,* lifted the lid and showed the bills still inside.

"That is quite a bit of money for a boy to have," Tio said, and there was a questioning note to his voice.

"It belongs to my people," Tara explained. "I tried to tell you about it when we first talked. I sold the lot of *rebozos* to one American lady. My people needed the money to buy food. It makes me feel sad that I could not get it to them."

"The time of the famine is passed," the doctor said soothingly. "I'm sure your people made out. Your parents must have earned more money from the sale of their wares in the market."

"*Sí!*" Tara agreed. "The *lacas* are so beautiful they would sell quickly. See how fine the workmanship is."

He picked up the precious *tecomate* and held it high, pointing to the golden bird.

The doctor took the bowl and studied it. "It is lovely," he said, "and I can see that the workmanship is very good, although I know nothing about such things. I will try to find someone who is an expert on lacquer ware. This bowl may prove to be a valuable clue to finding where your home is, even though fine pottery is made all over Mexico."

At his words a wave of homesickness swept through Tara. "I hope it will help to find my people," he said. Then feeling that the good doctor might think him ungrateful, he looked up quickly, but the great man's eyes were understanding.

"That will come later, though," the doctor said. "These things take time and we cannot tell how long it will take us to find your people. Also, I don't want you to leave us just yet. I don't think you are ready."

At Tara's questioning look he went on. "I told you I thought you would be one of our special ones. But you have more to learn. I want you to see enough of the new ways of living so that you can go back to your village and share with the people what is good in the new, yet still have them hold to what is best in the old — such as the fine craftsmanship of this bowl and your serape. Those things must never die, and it is sad that poverty has killed much of what was good in the old — the pride and dignity and self-respect."

"But when will I ever see my people?" These words came from Tara in a wail.

The doctor put a hand on Tara's shoulder. "It will not be too long, my son. I will have one of my helpers try to trace every clue that might lead to where you came from. Meantime, I want to take you to my home to live for a while. I have a son a little older than you. A private teacher lives with us. You and my boy will be good for each other — you can teach each other a lot."

The doctor's home was beautiful beyond anything Tara could have imagined. There was furniture covered with rich fabrics. Thick carpets under his feet made Tara's steps noiseless. He was shown the kitchen with its expanses of gleaming white, where water too hot to touch came from a tap. Where a tall white box held squares of ice, and enough food to keep his family for a year. He thought of how his mother carried water for miles — and carried the dirty clothing such a long way to wash on a stone beside a pool. Such miracles as he found here could never be for them — yet, perhaps if he learned much and worked hard he could in time buy many things for his mother to lighten her burdens — and to make her life more pleasant. His brain was awhirl with the strange new thoughts the doctor had planted there — with all the marvels of this new world.

He was made to take a bath every day beneath a shower and to wash his hands and face before each meal. In time he learned to enjoy the feeling of cleanliness. He liked himself better.

The doctor and his beautiful *señora* had five children: Rodolfo, a little older than Tara, Maria, a little more than a year younger, a boy five, a girl three, and a new baby.

Tara was to do chores about the place, run errands for the cook and housekeeper, wash the doctor's shiny car, and mow and trim the lawn. Every morning for two hours he went into the schoolroom with Rodolfo and Maria.

Feeling painfully self-conscious, he entered the schoolroom for the first time and stood before Señor Beto Nava, the teacher, who, he had been told, was an Indian like himself, picked up by the doctor, and educated. Later he had gone to the university in Mexico and had also attended college in the United States.

The teacher instantly won Tara's friendship by putting forth his hand and saying in the Indian fashion, "I give you good morning, Tara. It gives us pleasure to have you with us. Sit over there at the desk beside Rodolfo."

Tara darted a quick look at Rodolfo as he went to his seat. He resembled his handsome father, having the same glossy black hair, the straight long nose and firm mouth and chin. He bowed slightly as Tara sat down. Maria, however, flashed him a friendly and mischievous grin.

Tara did not know how to conduct himself with Rodolfo. A sudden realization of his terrible loneliness swept over him and he thought of Lucio and Pepe, of

Diablo, and of his family to whom he was important and wanted. How good it would be to be friends with this fine-looking boy. Yet, he knew that he was a servant in this home in which Rodolfo was a master. So, he must leave any gestures of friendship to the older boy, who no doubt looked down upon him.

He forgot to be concerned over this matter when Señor Nava commenced to speak. At once Tara felt that gateways to new knowledge were opening before him. He tried pinning each fact down hard in his mind so that he would never forget it. These were the things he would someday pass on to Marina and the little ones as they grew up — and maybe to Pepe and others like him who might be willing to listen.

A Fork in the Trail

Now the days were never long enough. Rodolfo and Maria watched the clock on the wall, which told when they would be released from the schoolroom, but the hours passed too fast for Tara. There was so much to learn, so many books still to read. He must hurry, because he had decided that when the "vacation" the two Brito children talked about came, he would set out to find his parents. He had not talked to the doctor about his plan, because he saw little of the busy man except as he came and went about the big house.

Tara ate in the kitchen with Rosa, the good-natured cook, Pedro, the gardener, García, the chauffeur, and Juanita, the housekeeper. They were a happy lot and there was always much joking and laughter while they ate. And such food! Tara had never tasted the like. There were of course *tortillas, enchiladas,* and red beans simmered over a slow fire in a thick sauce rich with chile. Such things were the staple foods of Mexico, but besides these there was meat every day,

and each Sunday there was turkey or chicken *mole* —
that delicious dish Tara had tasted only once before in
his life — when some important member of the family
had a wedding. Morning and evening there was cin-
namon-flavored hot chocolate twirled into foam by
a carved wooden whirler. Every day the noon and
evening meals were finished off with what was called
dessert — some delicious fruit or fluffy pudding or
ice cream. At every meal *pan dulces,* or sweet bread,
was served.

Tara was seldom by himself these days, but he had
never been lonelier. All of his associations were with
grown people. He seldom saw Rodolfo and Maria
except in the schoolroom. Although they lived in
the same house, they were of separate worlds. Tara
had been happier, really, living at the Boys' Club, for
there he had been with many companions his own age
and it had been fun being a shoeshine boy on the
busy streets of the Great City. Yet he would not have
traded this life for that one. The things he was learning, the facts he was storing in his mind, the riches of
books were something beyond price. However, he
could scarcely wait for the time to come when he
would set out to try to find his people.

He felt guilty about this yearning to go back to his
family — as though he were being disloyal and ungrateful to the good doctor who had shown him so
much.

One day the teacher sent Tara into one of the

family rooms for a book. The doctor's *señora* was there holding her baby and feeding it from a bottle. He stared at the baby so wistfully that she asked him to come closer and look at it.

"When I left home there was a little one about this size," he remarked.

"When you get home again," she said in her kindly manner, "he will likely be running around."

"If he has not been laid away in the City of the Dead like the others," Tara said.

She looked up quickly. "How many others?"

"Six," he said. "Six that I know of. There may have been others before I was born."

"It is wicked — wicked," she cried out.

"Yes," Tara agreed. "It is wicked that the Evil Eye is laid on helpless babes. My father shoots firecrackers in our house every morning and evening to scare away the bad spirits."

"Tara!" she cried impatiently. "Have you learned nothing during the months you have been here? There is no Evil Eye — no bad spirits except our own ignorance. That is what you must take back to your people. Shooting firecrackers won't keep your mother's babies from dying. But keeping the baby clean — allowing nothing to go into its mouth for the first year that has not been boiled — will save the lives of most of them."

"Have you not laid any babies away in the City of the Dead?" he asked.

"Certainly not. It's very simple to keep everything that goes into a baby's mouth clean. Filth kills our native babies — not an Evil Eye."

"I will tell my mother and our friends that," Tara said. "But they may not believe it."

"Ask them to try," the *señora* said. "They can at least do that, and I'm sure that some babies will be saved."

The next day the teacher talked about the olden days of Mexico, the remarkable civilizations of the Mayans and the Aztecs — their wonderful craftsmanship, their use of a calendar and of an alphabet. He said, "Then the Spanish conquerors came. They made slaves of the natives, took away their pride and dignity and their self-respect — qualities that they never regained . . ."

"But my people did not submit," Tara cried out. "They fled to the mountains rather than let themselves become slaves."

The teacher looked at Tara searchingly. "Your people did?" he asked.

Tara nodded.

"There was but one race who did not submit," the teacher said slowly. "The Tarascans — a proud and noble people. Are you a Tarascan?"

Tara nodded again, his heart beating fast. "I am called Tara because of that," he said. "In my veins runs the blood of kings."

"That is a valuable clue to where your home may

be found," the teacher said. "The Tarascans are
somewhat scattered, of course, but most of them live
in Michoacán. Many are found in Uruapan, where
beautiful lacquer is made."

"My people make fine lacquer ware," Tara cried.

"Does the name Uruapan awaken any memories?"
the teacher asked.

Tara shook his head.

Señor Nava mentioned several other names, but
they awakened no response in Tara's memory. Hope,
which had flamed for a moment, faded again.

"Don't worry," the teacher said. "The fact that
you are a Tarascan is the most important clue. It nar-
rows down our search a great deal. I feel that we are
beginning to get somewhere at last. We'll go on with
our lessons now, but tonight we'll discuss the matter
with Doctor Brito and perhaps we can figure out where
you are from."

It was difficult for Tara to keep his mind on his
studies for the rest of that day. The hours dragged
by slowly, but at last it was evening and he was sum-
moned into the doctor's library. Señor Nava was
there with Dr. Brito.

"So — you are a Tarascan?" the doctor said. "Knowing that is a big help. You are sure the name Michoacán means nothing to you?"

Tara shook his head.

"That is the name of a state. Many Tarascans live
there, although some live elsewhere, of course. You

said you lived by a big lake. And you cannot remember the name of the lake?"

Again Tara had to shake his head. "We call it just the lake," he said.

"Do you remember the name of the village near which you live?"

"Some call it the City of Kings. Others call it the Place of the Humming Birds. It is a small place, but it has a fine cathedral."

"That description fits hundreds of places," the teacher said. "Search your memory, Tara. How is the lake or the village different from other places?"

"I have not seen many other places," Tara replied, "except those we passed through on our long journey here to the Great City. We passed through many *poblados,* most of them larger than ours on the lake. Most of our villagers are fishermen. There are many islands in the lake — "

Then he straightened up. "One of the islands has a huge statue," he said. "I don't remember what they call it — but it is some great hero."

The teacher leaned forward. "Is the island named Janitzio?" he asked.

"We don't call places by special names," Tara said slowly. "We call it the Big Island of the Fishermen. All along its shore are the big nets they use."

"Ah!" The word came in triumph from the teacher. "At last we may be getting someplace. What sort of nets are they? What do they look like?"

"When the men are out on the lake with their nets spread out in two loops, they look like giant dragon-flies."

The doctor and teacher looked at each other. "That would be Lake Pátzcuaro," Señor Nava cried. "In no other place on earth do men use those butterfly nets. That is it!"

"I have heard that name," Tara said. "Long ago, it was. But I do remember hearing it." His heart was beating fast.

"But the butterfly fishing nets," the doctor said. "Why did you not tell us of those before? That would have cleared the matter up immediately."

"I thought that everywhere men fished that way," Tara said.

"Of course. How would you know?"

Silence fell over the comfortable room; there was no sound save the crackling of the fire. Tara, staring into its bright depths, wondered about his future, and knowing at last where his parents were gave him new hope. But why were the two men silent for so long? Tara wanted to cry out, to ask if Tio were going to send him home. If so, how soon?

As though he had read his mind the doctor asked, "Do you wish to be sent home at once, Tara? Or can you wait another week until school is over? I hope you can wait that long, because if you do, Señor Nava can take you in my car. And Rodolfo could go along. I want your teacher to see what they are doing for our people at the school the United Nations has set up there at Pátzcuaro."

Tara gulped. The urge to get back to his parents was almost overpowering. But he did not want to seem ungrateful for all that Tio had done for him. Besides, now he knew where they were. It would be wonderful traveling back in a big automobile — and with Señor Nava and Rodolfo.

There was a long silence while he thought over the matter. Finally he said slowly, "I will wait for the end of school. It will not be long."

"I knew that you wouldn't want to miss the examinations," the teacher said with a twinkle in his eyes.

That night Tara slept scarcely at all.

A Dream Come True

THE NEXT FEW DAYS dragged for Tara until the close of the school year. His hungry mind still absorbed information and he studied harder than ever so that he could learn as much as possible, yet the thought of his parents brought such a longing for them and his home that he could hardly stand it. He dreamed of them nearly every night now, and Diablo was always in those dreams.

At last, the day for their departure came. The previous night the back of the big automobile had been filled with boxes of books for him to take with him, so that he could continue his reading and learning.

"You have the key to all knowledge now," the teacher told him. "You can read. Every book should open a new gateway for you. To what use you put this key depends upon you from now on."

"I will go to the village school every day," Tara told him. "I shall never find another teacher such as you. But I will never forget the things you have taught me."

"Spread those things around, Tara," said the doctor, who had come to the gate to bid him farewell. "Make your life count for something by bettering the lot of your people. Never forget that we recognize in you one of our special ones. Go back to your family. You are still a boy. Finish out your boyhood. Then perhaps someday you will hunger for further learning. Perhaps you will go to the school of the United Nations in Pátzcuaro so you can be prepared to be a leader of men."

Tara clasped the doctor's hand and there was mist

in his eyes and a lump in his throat. "I can never thank you," he choked. "There are not enough words."

He had already said goodbye to Señor Brito and the younger children. Rodolfo was to go with them. This long ride in such luxury was in itself a great thrill to Tara. Along the road were the same sights he had seen on his way to the Great City: the loaded burros — the men themselves loaded and bent under heavy burdens — the women floating in their smooth, graceful way of walking beneath the heavy baskets which they carried on their heads — the boy goatherds — the oxen plowing the fields with crude wooden plows — the young men on bicycles. And at every stream or pond — wherever there was water, women were bent over scrubbing dirty clothes against rocks. They looked like the same women bent at the same tasks as when Tara had journeyed in the opposite direction. These patient people waiting beside the road for the ancient buses might  have been the same people he saw before. The first time he had seen them, though, he was part of that parade, staring wistfully at the shiny cars which sped by. Now, here he was in one of those cars.

The familiar mountains were like giant shoulders against the sky, and on their sides and in the valleys were small farms and men and women toiling — toiling.

Tara shook his head slowly and said, "I had forgotten how primitive is the way in which my people live. My heart now goes out in pity to them, for they must slave so hard and so long merely to keep alive from one day to the next."

Beto Nava gave him a searching look. "I had hoped

you would feel that way," he said. "The doctor and I have tried to plant a seed in your mind that will someday flower and bear fruit to help your people."

Tara frowned as he tried to puzzle the meaning of these words. They sounded like one of the riddles of the Wise One.

Rodolfo chuckled. "He means that he wants you to be a teacher when you grow up. My father and Señor Nava want all of those they call their special ones to become teachers in their own villages."

"Is that your meaning?" Tara turned to the man.

"It would not disappoint me," he said. "And I believe that you will find it will satisfy your heart if you can help to wipe out the poverty and ignorance of your people. I plan to stay a month in Pátzcuaro, where a tremendous social experiment designed to reduce poverty and illiteracy has begun. Twenty Tarascan villages, so far by-passed by most of man's improvements, have become a United Nations laboratory for teachers dedicated to stamping out misery in depressed rural nations."

"Then — " the hope was too great almost to be spoken, "perhaps you would come as a teacher to our village?"

"It might be," Señor Nava said. "Who knows? I will go where I am sent — where the need is greatest. But it could well be your village."

Tara began to bounce up and down on the seat. "Then I will go to school every day. I will study harder than anyone ever studied before. I will help you teach the slow ones. I will — what do you call it — dedicate myself to be the teacher. . . ."

Rodolfo and Beto Nava both burst out laughing. "Slow down! Slow down!" the man said. "Too many promises made at once might be hard to keep. You'd better think about your own future for a while. You're still a boy."

"I must be a doctor," Rodolfo said. "My father has planned it so. He wants me to carry on the work of caring for the Forgotten Ones when he gets old."

"I do not like the words 'Forgotten Ones.' " Tara frowned. "I was lost, but I have never been forgotten. I know it. My people have longed for me as I have for them."

"I'm sure of it, Tara," Señor Nava said. "But there are many waifs wandering the streets of the Great City who are actually abandoned because their parents are too poor to take care of them. That is why our beloved Tio goes out on the streets every night searching in alleys and doorways for the lost ones. I was one of them." His expression darkened. "But perhaps it was for the best. He educated me. Inspired me to dedicate my life to uplifting our people. He has helped hundreds of boys — has saved them from becoming beggars and thieves and has made useful citizens of them. He is a great man, our Tio."

"*Sí.* He is," Tara agreed. He turned to Rodolfo. "And you will be like him."

"I hope I can," the boy said. "I'll try. But perhaps I'd better change the name my father calls his lost boys. I didn't mean to hurt your feelings by calling you one of the Forgotten Ones."

"The boys aren't all abandoned," the teacher broke in. "Many of them are like Tara; they came in from remote portions of the country and became separated from parents who could not speak Spanish, so had no way of locating their lost children. Some become lost by wandering off from home. Tio manages to return many lost youngsters to their parents."

They rode in silence for a time. Tara enjoyed the scenery, but his thoughts were about his home and his loved ones.

Finally Rodolfo said, "I hope I didn't hurt your feelings, Tara."

"Of course not." Tara was surprised. His thoughts had been far away.

"I wish that I could be your friend," Rodolfo went on. "But you hold yourself off from me."

Tara looked at the other boy in surprise. "I did not hold myself off," he protested. "We were far apart because you were master and I was servant."

"But I never felt that way about you," Rodolfo cried. "I wanted to be friends but I thought you didn't like me."

Tara sighed at the thought of so many days of lost friendship because of lack of understanding.

"I was so lonely I could scarcely stand it," he said in a low voice.

Beto Nava spoke up. "Our Doctor Brito is very wise. He saw that you two boys would be good for each other. Rodolfo has a good mind, but he has a tendency to be lazy. When he saw how eager you were to learn, Tara, he got down to work and began to appreciate his advantages. And through each other you have both had glimpses into another world. I'm glad to see that at last the barrier between you has crumbled."

Tara sat there in silence watching the countryside slide by. So Rodolfo was his friend! It gave him a good warm feeling.

Tara had forgotten how many turns of the sun it had taken for him and his parents to walk to the Great City. Now it was not yet evening and they were already at the place called Pátzcuaro. The cobbled streets and the plaza were familiar.

"Is this it?" Beto Nava asked. "Is this where your people live?"

Tara shook his head. "No. But we passed through here on our way to the Great City. I think — I am sure I could find my way from here. The lake is in that direction." He pointed.

"The lake!"

Rodolfo laughed. "Do you intend to swim?"

"No. But perhaps there will be a fishing boat to take

me to the village. Nearly every day someone comes from one of the fishing villages to where this road touches the lake."

"Can't we get to your village by car?" Señor Nava asked.

Tara turned to the teacher with a regretful expression. "I forgot to tell you," he cried. "There is no way to get there by car. There is only a narrow trail for walking — or for burros. Or the way by boat. There is no road to my village. And only a faint trail from there to my home."

"We could walk," Rodolfo cried.

"It is far," Tara said. "And what about my books? They are too heavy to carry on my back. And I will not leave them. They are my treasures."

"We will manage," the teacher said. "We will drive the car to the dock and hire a boat to take us to your

village. Then you can walk to your home and bring
your burros to carry the books."

"Yes," Tara cried eagerly. "That will be the way.
Diablo will be there. Yes, I am very sure he will be
there. He must be. He is the smartest and strongest
burro in the world. He can carry my books from the
boat."

"You and your Diablo!" Rodolfo laughed.

There was no end to the amazing things that kept
happening to Tara. At the place where the boats
landed was the one in which Pedro had put the motor
from an old automobile to make a "putt-putt" boat
of it.

The boxes of books were loaded and the boat sped
across the water, causing the white herons to rise in
graceful clouds. This ride was in itself an adventure.
The lake was deserted of duck hunters and butterfly
net fishermen. Tara had half hoped to see Lucio on
the lake, although he knew it was not the time of day
for fishing or hunting.

They sped toward the island of the big statue. Its
gigantic whiteness loomed against the blue sky and
the great arm seemed upraised in welcome to Tara.

"Tell the boatman, Tara, where the village is."
Beto Nava's words brought Tara back to reality.

Tara pointed to the direction in which it lay. "It is
the Place of the Humming Birds," he said.

The boatman nodded. "As if I didn't know your
village." He grinned.

The boat pulled up to the shore alongside a row
of crude dugouts. Tara's heart fluttered at the familiar
sight.

At first, there was was no one to be seen, but by the
time the boatman had tied the craft to a post, the shore
was swarming with boys and girls.

"Tara! Tara!" they cried. "You have come back!

We thought you were lost for ever."

Some of them stared unashamedly at the teacher and Rodolfo in their neat, clean clothes. Then some of them shoved out greedy, dirty hands and chanted, "Cincos! Cincos!"

"No! No!" Tara cried, shoving them away. "These people are not tourists. They are my friends. You shame me with your begging."

The boys and girls ceased their chant, but looked at Tara in surprise.

"Help me," Tara said as he tried to lift one of the boxes of books. Then he set it down again and stared at the native boys and girls who were his people. A new thought had struck him. He turned to Señor Nava.

"These books are treasures," he said slowly. "They open new worlds and new adventures. But I would be selfish to keep them just for myself. Perhaps I will keep one or two as my own — but I should like to put the rest in the village school so that others may enjoy them. Would the good doctor mind?"

The teacher's eyes shone. "I am sure the good doctor would be very pleased."

"Then," Tara cried, opening the boxes. "Help me, my friends. We will carry the precious books to the school. And do not ask for cincos for doing this work. The books belong to all of us. You are but helping yourselves."

The books were carried by willing arms and placed

on the nearly empty shelves of the schoolroom.

"Would you walk with me to my home?" Tara asked shyly when all of the books had been placed. "It is humble and poor — but I want you to meet my people."

Rodolfo and the teacher gave each other meaning looks that Tara could not understand. Perhaps they did not want to go with him.

Then the teacher said, "Of course we want to go, Tara. We wish to meet your people."

They walked up the steep winding path until they reached the huddle of adobe houses. The camelina was in full bloom, as were the other red and pink flowers. The Wise One sat in the shade carefully wielding his sharp etching tool. The Good One sat just inside the doorway weaving. Inside the room in which the cooking and eating were done Tara heard the familiar *slap-slap* of *tortillas* being made, and the smell of their cooking made his mouth water. It was as though he had never left.

At that moment Marina came from the door with a water jar on her shoulder. "Tara!" she cried and, setting down the jar, she threw herself at him.

Cheran rushed from the door and Zolic and Kalli looked up in surprise, then they too came toward him. Tara thought he would be smothered, his mother hugged him so hard and her tears fell on him like rain.

The warmth of their love enveloped him.

Finally he remembered Beto Nava and Rodolfo,

and he drew them forward to present to his family. "These are my good friends," he said.

The women curtsied and the Old One touched the teacher's hand in a gesture of gratitude, but there was the barrier of language between them. The teacher tried to talk to them in the language of his own Indian race. But it was a different tongue and he could not make himself understood.

"Ah, my son!" Cheran cried. "How we have worried about you! We waited and waited at the market place. But there was no way of finding you. We hoped that you might have set out for home already. How our hearts have ached for you."

A great lump choked Tara's throat. How good it was to belong to a family who loved him. How terrible it would be to be a Forgotten One.

"I beg you to be seated. The women will bring refreshments." Zolic made a gesture of hospitality to the guests, motioning to the worn rocks around the patio which had served as seats for generations of his family.

Señor Nava and Rodolfo sat down. The women hurried away to prepare refreshments. Tara looked around him eagerly. There was a small toddler who clung to Marina's skirt and peered around shyly with wide round eyes. So this was the little one Marina had carried in her *rebozo!* Tara would have to make friends with the little fellow.

Again he looked around him — anxiously this time.

"Your good father is away gathering wood," Zolic said in answer to his look.

"Then," Tara said, "Diablo must be with him."

"That Diablo!" Zolic exclaimed. "Who can say where he is?"

At those words Tara's hopes crumbled. He had counted so on finding Diablo. Probably, then, someone had stolen him at the edge of the Great City. And his parents had never found him.

His mother and grandmother came bearing a tray of *tortillas* with freshly cut oranges and cooling *jicamas,* which they passed to the guests. Tara sat on a stone and tried to make polite conversation in spite of the worry that was eating his heart. He was proud of the courteous manners of his people. It was pleasant and beautiful here in the shade of the ancient trees with flowers everywhere and the scent of mimosas filling the air.

"You have a charming home, Tara," the teacher said. "And your people are good and industrious. I can understand why you were so eager to come back."

"You can see," Tara said with a touch of pride, "that I was never one of the Forgotten Ones."

"Of course not," Señor Nava said. "That term should never apply to you. You are right to resent it. Your family love and cherish you. I am sorry your father is not here."

He rose and Rodolfo did, too. "It is getting late," Señor Nava said. "We will miss our boat ride back to

Pátzcuaro if we do not hurry. I must make arrangements for my stay at the United Nations school. Besides, you have much to say to your family."

"But I will see you again? You, Señor Nava, will perhaps come to teach our village school? And you, Rodolfo — it would be wonderful if you could stay here for a while. But of course my home is too crude for you to enjoy."

A great smile broke out on Rodolfo's handsome face. "How I've been hoping that you would ask me. I already have permission from my father to stay here while Señor Nava is in Pátzcuaro — that is, if you want me."

"IF I want you! How could I want anything more?" Tara turned to his mother and asked quickly if she minded if Rodolfo stayed.

She did not mind, as he knew she would not. The hospitality of the Olinas was unbounded.

"I can't tell you," the teacher said, "how eager he was for your invitation. But tonight we will spend in Pátzcuaro. After all, his bag with his clothes is there in the car. Tomorrow he can come back on the boat."

"We will go duck shooting. We will fish with the butterfly nets. We will go on long exploring trips into the mountains . . ." the eager words tumbled from Tara's lips.

Rodolfo's eyes shone.

"I will walk back with you to the boat," Tara cried. "Then," he turned to his mother and the others, "I will hurry back to tell you of all that has happened to me."

He stood watching the white boat that carried his friends through the water until it grew small in the distance. As he turned to go up the trail he saw his Uncle Lucio watching him, one foot on the dugout canoe. There was a smile on his handsome face. He still looked like one of the gods of old.

"Lucio!" Tara cried happily. "I am so glad to see you."

"And *I*'m glad to see you, my young rooster," Lucio said in his deep, familiar voice. "I feared that our Restless One was lost forever. But you are back. And you have changed. You look the same, yet different. I cannot say just how. Did you find what you were looking for, young friend?"

Tara turned his head slightly so that he was staring at the lake, now reflecting the glow of sunset. Had he found what he was looking for? Suddenly, it came to him like a quick blaze of light, for a single moment illuminating his mind — making the meaning of things clear.

He turned to Lucio and said quietly. "Yes. I found it. But it is nothing I can show you. It is something inside myself."

Lucio looked puzzled. Tara could not explain. He felt that this inner feeling was something his uncle would not understand. Yet there would always be the comfortable, happy sensation when they were together. It was good to be together again.

Tara said, "My friend is coming back to stay with me for a month. Will you help me show him how to shoot the ducks with the *atl-atl* and to catch fish with the butterfly nets?"

"Yes, my young rooster," Lucio said, giving Tara his lazy smile. "I have missed you greatly. It will be pleasant to have you and your guest for company."

Tara turned and raced up the trail toward his home. "Old ways are good," his heart sang. "And so are the new. Take what is best of both, and happiness will come to you."

Panting, Tara reached his home. His family was still grouped as he had left them — all of them talking at once about his return. His father was there to give him a joyful embrace, and Tlaka acted as if he were about to devour him. The group was complete except for Diablo. Tara did not have it in his heart to ask more about him now when everyone was so happy.

He removed the folded serape which he carried over his right shoulder and bowed before his grandmother. "This beautiful serape kept me warm when I most needed it," he said. "I give you my thanks for such a gift. I will treasure it always."

Then with a triumphant gesture he drew out the golden bird *tecomate* from beneath his shirt and ceremoniously handed it to his mother. "Lift the lid," he said.

A cry of delight came from her lips as she drew out the bills. "So much money!" she cried. "Never have I seen so much at one time. How did you get it?"

"It is such a long story," he said with a quirked smile, "and my stomach begs for your good *tortillas*. I will talk while I eat."

"For certain, you are hungry!" she cried and instantly she, the grandmother, and Marina all hurried to get his simple meal ready.

While they worked and later while they ate in the sweet-smelling patio, he told them of his accident and of the strange and wonderful things that had happened to him since. He glanced at the golden-bird gourd on the shelf where his mother had placed it. The lines of the golden bird caught the glint of the charcoal fire.

"You were right, my good mother," he said turning to her. "You said that the golden bird would lead me to good fortune — to my heart's desire. My mind is crammed with so many things — and I do not have words to say them . . ."

He paused. How could he explain his thoughts, that he believed, now, this golden bird stood for what was good in the old ways — the main thing his people must hold to, their artistic craftsmanship — but that also he had discovered much good in the new ways. He realized that he was not wise enough to explain it just yet, and he knew it would be foolish to start Zolic off on one of his loud arguments.

Instead Tara decided that now it would not seem rude for him to inquire if they had ever heard anything about Diablo.

"It makes my heart glad, my father and mother," he said, "that you reached home from the Great City safely. But I miss my friend, Diablo. I would like to choke the thief who stole him."

"The thief who would steal Diablo — " his father cried out, then broke off speaking and bent his head. Silence fell over the little group — a strange silence that Tara was at a loss to understand.

From behind Tara came a snuffing noise. A weight pressed on his shoulder, coarse hair brushed his cheek, and a welcome odor came to his nostrils — the good earthy odor of sweat and dust and animal, which was to Tara like the sweetest perfume.

He turned his head and there was Diablo's head resting on his shoulder with that silly, happy expression. Tara threw his arms about the shaggy neck and buried his face behind the burro's ear.

"Diablo! Diablo!" The glad words choked his throat. "You weren't lost. You weren't stolen."

"He was with me." His father chuckled. "As I was

saying, the thief who would steal Diablo would have
a sorry bargain. We found him waiting outside the
city. He will carry me and work for me every day, but
for no one else. He hasn't forgotten his trick of sitting
down. Every morning he has turned his face toward

the Great City and let out that giant bray, for all the world as though calling you."

Tara's arms tightened and he raised his head to gaze happily upon this most unusual animal. Diablo rolled back his upper lip in the same old grin and let out a resounding *he-haw*.

Tara was certain that Diablo understood every word that had been said, and his heart flooded with happiness. This, he was sure, was the most perfect day of his life.